THE COMING OF CUCULAIN

STANDISH O'GRADY

The Coming of Cuculain

Standish O' Grady

© 1st World Library – Literary Society, 2004
PO Box 2211
Fairfield, IA 52556
www.1stworldlibrary.org
First Edition

LCCN: 2004195355

Softcover ISBN: 1-4218-0189-2
Hardcover ISBN: 1-4218-0089-6
eBook ISBN: 1-4218-0289-9

Purchase *"The Coming of Cuculain"*
as a traditional bound book at:
www.1stWorldLibrary.org/purchase.asp?ISBN=1-4218-0189-2

1st World Library Literary Society is a nonprofit organization dedicated to promoting literacy by:

- Creating a free internet library accessible from any computer worldwide.
- Hosting writing competitions and offering book publishing scholarships.

**Readers interested in supporting literacy
through sponsorship, donations or
membership please contact:
literacy@1stworldlibrary.org
Check us out at: www. 1stworldlibrary.ORG
and start downloading free ebooks today.**

PREFACE

There are three great cycles of Gaelic literature. The first treats of the gods; the second of the Red Branch Knights of Ulster and their contemporaries; the third is the so-called Ossianic. Of the Ossianic, Finn is the chief character; of the Red Branch cycle, Cuculain, the hero of our tale.

Cuculain and his friends are historical characters, seen as it were through mists of love and wonder, whom men could not forget, but for centuries continued to celebrate in countless songs and stories. They were not literary phantoms, but actual existences; imaginary and fictitious characters, mere creatures of idle fancy, do not live and flourish so in the world's memory. And as to the gigantic stature and superhuman prowess and achievements of those antique heroes, it must not be forgotten that all art magnifies, as if in obedience to some strong law; and so, even in our own times, Grattan, where he stands in artistic bronze, is twice as great as the real Grattan thundering in the Senate. I will therefore ask the reader, remembering the large manner of the antique literature from which our tale is drawn, to forget for a while that there is such a thing as scientific history, to give his imagination a holiday, and follow with kindly interest the singular story of the boyhood of Cuculain, "battle-prop of the valour and torch of the chivalry of the Ultonians."

I have endeavoured so to tell the story as to give a general idea of the cycle, and of primitive heroic Irish life as reflected in that literature, laying the cycle, so far as accessible, under contribution to furnish forth the tale. Within a short compass I would bring before swift modern readers the more striking aspects of a literature so vast and archaic as to repel all but students.

STANDISH O'GRADY

A TRIBUTE BY A. E.

In this age we read so much that we lay too great a burden on the imagination. It is unable to create images which are the spiritual equivalent of the words on the printed page, and reading becomes for too many an occupation of the eye rather than of the mind. How rarely - out of the multitude of volumes a man reads in his lifetime - can he remember where or when he read any particular book, or with any vividness recall the mood it evoked in him. When I close my eyes, and brood in memory over the books which most profoundly affected me, I find none excited my imagination more than Standish O'Grady's epical narrative of Cuculain. Whitman said of his Leaves of Grass, "Camerado, this is no book: who touches this touches a man" and O'Grady might have boasted of his Bardic History of Ireland, written with his whole being, that there was more than a man in it, there was the soul of a people, its noblest and most exalted life symbolised in the story of one heroic character.

With reference to Ireland, I was at the time I read like many others who were bereaved of the history of their race. I was as a man who, through some accident, had lost memory of his past, who could recall no more than a few months of new life, and could not say to what songs his cradle had been rocked, what mother had nursed him, who were the playmates of childhood or by what woods and streams he had wandered. When I read O'Grady I was as such a man who suddenly feels ancient memories rushing at him, and knows he was born in a royal house, that he had mixed with the mighty of heaven and earth and had the very noblest for his companions. It was the memory of race which rose up within me as I read, and I felt exalted as one who learns he is among the children of kings. That is what O'Grady did for me and for others who were my contemporaries, and I welcome these reprints of his tales in the hope that he will go on magically recreating for generations yet unborn the ancestral life of their race in Ireland. For many centuries the youth of Ireland as it grew up was made aware of the life of bygone ages, and there were always some who remade themselves in the heroic mould before they passed on. The sentiment engendered by the Gaelic literature was an arcane presence, though unconscious of itself, in those who for the past hundred years had learned another speech. In O'Grady's writings the submerged river of national culture rose up again, a shining torrent, and I realised as I bathed in that stream, that the greatest spiritual evil one nation could inflict on another was to cut off from it the story of the national soul. For not all music can be played upon any instrument, and human nature for most of us is like a harp on which can be rendered the music written for the harp but not that written for the violin. The harp strings quiver for the harp-player alone, and he who can utter his passion through the violin is silent before an unfamiliar instrument. That is why the Irish have rarely been deeply stirred by English literature though it is one of the great literatures of the world. Our history was different and the evolutionary product was a peculiarity of character, and the strings of our being vibrate most in ecstasy when the music evokes ancestral moods or embodies emotions akin to these. I am not going to argue the comparative worth of the Gaelic and English tradition. All I can say is that the traditions of our own country move us more than the traditions of any other. Even if there was not essential greatness in them we would love them for the same reasons which bring back so many exiles to revisit the haunts of childhood. But there was essential greatness in that neglected bardic literature which O'Grady was the first to reveal in a noble manner. He had the spirit of an ancient epic poet. He is a comrade of Homer, his birth delayed in time perhaps that he might renew for a sophisticated people the elemental simplicity and hardihood men had when the world was young and manhood was prized more than any of its parts, more than thought or beauty or feeling. He has created for us or rediscovered one figure which looms in the imagination as a high comrade of Hector, Achilles, Ulysses, Rama or Yudisthira, as great in spirit as any. Who could extol enough his Cuculain, that incarnation of Gaelic chivalry, the fire and gentleness, the beauty and heroic ardour or the imaginative splendour of the episodes in his retelling of the ancient story. There are writers who bewitch us by a magical use of words, whose lines glitter like jewels, whose effects are gained by an elaborate art and who deal with the subtlest emotions. Others again are simple as an Egyptian image and yet are more impressive and you remember them less for the sentence than for a grandiose effect. They are not so much concerned with the art of words as with the creation of great images informed with magnificence of spirit. They are not lesser artists but greater, for there is a greater art in the simplification of form in the statue of Memnon than there is in the intricate detail of a bronze by Benvenuto Cellini. Standish O'Grady had in his best moments that epic wholeness and simplicity, and the figure of Cuculain amid his companions of the Red Branch which he discovered and refashioned for us is I think the greatest spiritual gift any Irishman for centuries has given to Ireland.

I know it will be said that this is a scientific age, the world is so full of necessitous life that it is waste of time for young Ireland to brood upon tales of legendary heroes, who fought with enchanters, who harnessed wild fairy horses to magic chariots and who talked with the ancient gods, and that it would be much better for youth to be scientific and practical. Do not believe it, dear Irish boy, dear Irish girl. I know as well as any the economic needs of our people. They must not be overlooked, but keep still in your hearts some desires which might enter Paradise. Keep in your souls some images of magnificence so that hereafter the halls of heaven and the divine folk may not seem altogether alien to the spirit. These legends have passed the test of generations for century after century, and they were treasured and passed on to those who followed, and that was because there was something in them akin to the immortal spirit. Humanity cannot carry with it through time the memory of all its deeds and imaginations, and it burdens itself only in a new era with what was highest among the imaginations of the ancestors. What is essentially noble is never out of date. The figures carved by Phidias for the Parthenon still shine by the side of the greatest modern sculpture. There has been no evolution of the human form to a greater beauty than the ancient Greeks saw and the forms they carved are not strange to us, and if this is true of the outward form it is true of the indwelling spirit. What is essentially noble is contemporary with all that is splendid to-day, and, until the mass of men are equal in spirit, the great figures of the past will affect us less as memories than as prophecies of the Golden Age to which youth is ever hurrying in its heart.

O'Grady in his stories of the Red Branch rescued from the past what was contemporary to the best in us to-day, and he was equal in his gifts as a writer to the greatest of his bardic predecessors in Ireland. His sentences are charged with a heroic energy, and, when he is telling a great tale, their rise and fall are like the flashing and falling of the bright sword of some great champion in battle, or the onset and withdrawal of Atlantic surges. He can at need be beautifully tender and quiet. Who that has read his tale of the young Finn and the Seven Ancients will forget the weeping of Finn over the kindness of the famine-stricken old men, and their wonder at his weeping and the self-forgetful pathos of their meditation unconscious that it was their own sacrifice called forth the tears of Finn. "Youth," they said, "has many sorrows that cold age cannot comprehend."

There are critics repelled by the abounding energy in O'Grady's sentences. It is easy to point to faults due to excess and abundance, but how rare in literature is that heroic energy and power. There is something arcane and elemental in it, a quality that the most careful stylist cannot attain, however he uses the file, however subtle he is. O'Grady has noticed this power in the ancient bards and we find it in his own writing. It ran all through the Bardic History, the Critical and Philosophical History, and through the political books, "The Tory Democracy" and "All Ireland." There is this imaginative energy in the tale of Cuculain, in all its episodes, the slaying of the hound, the capture of the Laity Macha, the hunting of the enchanted deer, the capture of the wild swans, the fight at the ford and the awakening of the Red Branch. In the later tale of Red Hugh which he calls "The Flight of the Eagle" there is the same quality of power joined with a shining simplicity in the narrative which rises into a poetic ecstacy in that wonderful chapter where Red Hugh, escaping from the Pale, rides through the Mountain Gates of Ulster, and sees high above him Slieve Mullion, a mountain of the Gods, the birthplace of legend "more mythic than Avernus" and O'Grady evokes for us and his hero the legendary past, and the great hill seems to be like Mount Sinai, thronged with immortals, and it lives and speaks to the fugitive boy, "the last great secular champion of the Gael," and inspires him for the fulfilment of his destiny. We might say of Red Hugh and indeed of all O'Grady's heroes that they are the spiritual progeny of Cuculain. From Red Hugh down to the boys who have such enchanting adventures in "Lost on Du Corrig" and "The Chain of Gold" they have all a natural and hardy purity of mind, a beautiful simplicity of character, and one can imagine them all in an hour of need, being faithful to any trust like the darling of the Red Branch. These shining lads never grew up amid books. They are as much children of nature as the Lucy of Wordsworth's poetry. It might be said of them as the poet of the Kalevala sang of himself,

"Winds and waters my instructors."

These were O'Grady's own earliest companions and no man can find better comrades than earth, water, air and sun. I imagine O'Grady's own youth was not so very different from the youth of Red Hugh before his captivity; that he lived on the wild and rocky western coast, that he rowed in coracles, explored the caves, spoke much with hardy natural people, fishermen and workers on the land, primitive folk, simple in speech, but with that fundamental depth men have who are much in nature in companionship with the elements, the elder brothers of humanity: it must have been out of such a boyhood and such intimacies with natural and unsophisticated people that there came to him the understanding of the heroes of the Red Branch. How pallid, beside the ruddy chivalry who pass huge and fleet and bright through O'Grady's pages, appear Tennyson's bloodless Knights of the Round Table, fabricated in the study to be read in the drawing-room, as anaemic as Burne Jones' lifeless men in armour. The heroes of ancient Irish legend reincarnated in the mind of a man who could breathe into them the fire of life, caught from sun and wind, their ancient deities, and send them, forth to the world to do greater deeds, to act through many men and speak through many voices. What sorcery was in the Irish mind that it has taken so many years to win but a little recognition for this splendid spirit; and that others who came after him, who diluted the pure fiery wine of romance he gave us with literary water, should be as well known or more widely read. For my own part I can only point back to him and say whatever is Irish in me he kindled to life, and I am humble when I read his epic tale, feeling how much greater a thing it is for the soul of a writer to have been the habitation of a demigod than to have had the subtlest intellections.

We praise the man who rushes into a burning mansion and brings out its greatest treasure. So ought we to praise this man who rescued from the perishing Gaelic tradition its darling hero and restored him to us, and I think now that Cuculain will not perish, and he will be invisibly present at many a council of youth, and he will be the daring which lifts the will beyond itself and fires it for great causes, and he will also be the courtesy which shall overcome the enemy that nothing else may overcome.

I am sure that Standish O'Grady would rather I should speak of his work and its bearing on the spiritual life of Ireland, than about himself, and, because I think so, in this reverie I have followed no set plan but have let my thoughts run as they will. But I would not have any to think that this man was only a writer, or that he could have had the heroes of the past for spiritual companions, without himself being inspired to fight dragons and wizardy. I have sometimes regretted that contemporary politics drew O'Grady away from the work he began so greatly. I have said to myself he might have given us an Oscar, a Diarmuid or a Caoilte, an equal comrade to Cuculain, but he could not, being lit up by the spirit of his hero, be merely the bard and not the fighter, and no man in Ireland intervened in the affairs of his country with a superior nobility of aim. He was the last champion of the Irish aristocracy and still more the voice of conscience for them, and he spoke to them of their duty to the nation as one might imagine some fearless prophet speaking to a council of degenerate princes. When the aristocracy failed Ireland he bade them farewell, and wrote the epitaph of their class in words whose scorn we almost forget because of their sounding melody and beauty. He turned his mind to the problems of democracy and more especially of those workers who are trapped in the city, and he pointed out for them the way of escape and how they might renew life in the green fields close to Earth, their ancient mother and nurse. He used too exalted a language for those to whom he spoke to understand, and it might seem that all these vehement appeals had failed but that we know that what is fine never really fails. When a man is in advance of his age, a generation unborn when he speaks, is born in due time and finds in him its inspiration. O'Grady may have failed in his appeal to the aristocracy of his own time but he may yet create an aristocracy of character and intellect in Ireland. The political and social writings will remain to uplift and inspire and to remind us that the man who wrote the stories of heroes had a bravery of his own and a wisdom of his own. I owe so much to Standish O'Grady that I would like to leave it on record that it was he who made me conscious and proud of my country, and recalled my mind, that might have wandered otherwise over too wide and vague a field of thought, to think of the earth under my feet and the children of our common mother. There hangs in the Municipal Gallery of Dublin the portrait of a man with brooding eyes, and scrawled on the canvas is the subject of his bitter meditation, "The Lost Land." I hope that O'Grady will find before he goes back to Tir-na-noge that Ireland has found again through him what seemed lost for ever, the law of its own being, and its memories which go back to the beginning of the world.

CHAPTER I

THE RED BRANCH

"There were giants in the earth in those days, the same were mighty men which were of yore men of renown."

The Red Branch feasted one night in their great hall at Emain Macha. So vast was the hall that a man, such as men are now, standing in the centre and shouting his loudest, would not be heard at the circumference, yet the low laughter of the King sitting at one end was clearly audible to those who sat around the Champion at the other. The sons of Dithorba made it, giants of the elder time, labouring there under the brazen shoutings of Macha and the roar of her sounding thongs. Its length was a mile and nine furlongs and a cubit. With her brooch pin she ploughed its outline upon the plain, and its breadth was not much less. Trees such as the earth nourished then upheld the massy roof beneath which feasted that heroic brood, the great-hearted children of Rury, huge offspring of the gods and giants of the dawn of time. For mighty exceedingly were these men. At the noise of them running to battle all Ireland shook, and the illimitable Lir [Footnote: Lir was the sea-god, the Oceanns of the Celt; no doubt the same as the British Lear, the wild, white-headed old king, who had such singular daughters; two, monsters of cruelty, and one, exquisitely sweet, kind, and serene, viz.: Storm, Hurricane, and Calm.] trembled in his watery halls; the roar of their brazen chariots reverberated from the solid canopy of heaven, and their war-steeds drank rivers dry.

A vast murmur rose from the assembly, for like distant thunder or the far-off murmuring of agitated waters was the continuous hum of their blended conversation and laughter, while, ever and anon, cleaving the many-tongued confusion, uprose friendly voices, clearer and stronger than battle-trumpets, when one hero chall-enged another to drink, wishing him victory and success, and his words rang round the hollow dome. Innumerable candles, tall as spears, illuminated the scene. The eyes of the heroes sparkled, and their faces, white and ruddy, beamed with festal mirth and mutual affection. Their yellow hair shone. Their banqueting attire, white and scarlet, glowed against the outer gloom. Their round brooches and mantle-pins of gold, or silver, or golden bronze, their drinking vessels and instruments of festivity, flashed and glittered in the light. They rejoiced in their glory and their might, and in the inviolable amity in which they were knit together, a host of comrades, a knot of heroic valour and affection which no strength or cunning, and no power, seen or unseen, could ever relax or untie.

At one extremity of the vast hall, upon a raised seat, sat their young king, Concobar Mac Nessa, slender, handsome, and upright. A canopy of bronze, round as the bent sling of the Sun-god, the long-handed, far-shooting son of Ethlend, [Footnote: This was the god Lu Lam-fada, i.e., Lu, the Long-Handed. The rainbow was his sling. Remember that the rod sling, familiar enough now to Irish boys, was the weapon of the ancient Irish, and not the sling which is made of two cords.] encircled his head. At his right hand lay a staff of silver. Far away at the other end of the hall, on a raised seat, sat the Champion Fergus Mac Roy, like a colossus. The stars and clouds of night were round his head and shoulders seen through the wide and high entrance of the dun, whose doors no man had ever seen closed and barred. Aloft, suspended from the dim rafters, hung the naked forms of great men clear against the dark dome, having the cords of their slaughter around their necks and their white limbs splashed with blood. Kings were they who had murmured against the sovereignty of the Red Branch. Through the wide doorway out of the night flew a huge bird, black and grey, unseen, and soaring upwards sat upon the rafters, its eyes like burning fire. It was the Mor-Reega, [Footnote: There were three war goddesses: - (1) Badb (pronounced Byve); (2) Macha, already referred to; (3) The Mor-Rigu or Mor-Reega, who wag the greatest of the three.] or Great Queen, the far-striding terrible daughter of Iarnmas (Iron-Death). Her voice was like the shouting of ten thousand men. Dear to her were these heroes. More she rejoiced in them feasting than in the battle-prowess of the rest.

When supper was ended their bard, in his singing robes and girt around the temples with a golden fillet, stood up and sang. He sang how once a king of the Ultonians, having plunged into the sea-depths, there slew a monster which had wrought much havoc amongst fishers and seafaring men. The heroes attended to his song, leaning forward with bright eyes. They applauded the song and the singer, and praised the valour of the heroic man [Footnote: This was Fergus Mac Leda, Fergus, son of Leda, one of the more ancient kings of Ulster. His contest with the sea-monster is the theme of a heroic tale.] who had done that deed. Then the champion struck the table with his clenched hand, and addressed the assembly. Wrath and sorrow were in his voice. It resembled the brool of lions heard afar by seafaring men upon some savage shore on a still night.

"Famous deeds," he said, "are not wrought now amongst the Red Branch. I think we are all become women. I grow weary of these huntings in the morning and mimic exercises of war, and this training of steeds and careering of brazen chariots stained never with aught but dust and mire, and these unearned feastings at night and vain applause of the brave deeds of our forefathers. Come now, let us make an end of this. Let us conquer Banba [Footnote: One of Ireland's many names.] wholly in all her green borders, and let the realms of Lir, which sustain no foot of man, be the limit of our sovereignty. Let us gather the tributes of all Ireland, after many battles and much warlike toil. Then more sweetly shall we drink while the bards chaunt our own prowess. Once I knew a coward who boasted endlessly about his forefathers, and at last my anger rose, and with a flat hand I slew him in the middle of his speech, and paid no eric, for he was nothing. We have the blood of heroes in our veins, and we sit here nightly boasting about them; about Rury, whose name we bear, being all his children; and Macha the warrioress, who brought hither bound the sons of Dithorba and made them rear this mighty dun; and Combat son of Fiontann; and my namesake Fergus,[Footnote: This was the king already referred to who slew the sea-monster. The monster had left upon him that mark and memorial of the struggle.] whose crooked mouth was no dishonour, and the rest of our hero sires; and we consume the rents and tributes of Ulster which they by their prowess conquered to us, and which flow hither in abundance from every corner of the province. Valiant men, too, will one day come hither and slay us as I slew that boaster, and here in Emain Macha their bards will praise them. Then in the halls of the dead shall we say to our sires, 'All that you got for us by your blood and your sweat that have we lost, and the glory of the Red Branch is at an end.'"

That speech was pleasing to the Red Branch, and they cried out that Fergus Mac Roy had spoken well. Then all at once, on a sudden impulse, they sang the battle-song of the Ultonians, and shouted for the war so that the building quaked and rocked, and in the hall of the weapons there was a clangour of falling shields, and men died that night for extreme dread, so mightily shouted the Ultonians around their king and around Fergus. When the echoes and reverberations of that shout ceased to sound in the vaulted roof and in the far recesses and galleries, then there arose somewhere upon the night a clear chorus of treble voices, singing, too, the war-chant of the Ultonians, as when rising out of the clangour of brazen instruments of music there shrills forth the clear sound of fifes. For the immature scions of the Red Branch, boys and tender youths, awakened out of slumber, heard them, and from remote dormitories responded to their sires, and they cried aloud together and shouted. The trees of Ulster shed their early leaves and buds at that shout, and birds fell dead from the branches.

Concobar struck the brazen canopy with his silver rod. The smitten brass rang like a bell, and the Ultonians in silence hearkened for the words of their clear-voiced king.

Standish O'Grady

"No ruler of men," he said, "however masterful and imperious, could withstand this torrent of martial ardour which rolls to-night through the souls of the children of Rury, still less I, newly come to this high throne, having been but as it were yesterday your comrade and equal, till Fergus, to my grief, resigned the sovereignty, and caused me, a boy, to be made king of Ulla and captain of the Red Branch. But now I say, ere we consider what province or territory shall first see the embattled Red Branch cross her borders, let us enquire of Cathvah the Ard-Druid, whether the omens be propitious, and whether through his art he is able to reveal to us some rite to be performed or prohibition to be observed."

That proposal was not pleasing to Fergus, but it pleased the Red Branch, and they praised the wisdom of their king.

Then Cathvah the Ard-Druid [Footnote: High Druid, or Chief Druid. Similarly we have Ard-Ri or High King.] spake.

"It hath been foretold," he said, "long since, that the Ultonians shall win glory such as never was and never will be, and that their fame shall endure till the world's end. But, first, there are prophecies to be accomplished and predictions to be fulfilled. For ere these things may be there shall come a child to Emain Macha, attended by clear portents from the gods; through him shall arise our deathless fame. Also it hath been foretold that there shall be great divisions and fratricidal strife amongst the children of Rury, a storm of war which shall strip the Red Branch nigh bare."

Fergus was wroth at this, and spoke words of scorn

concerning the diviner, and concerning all omens, prohibitions, and prophecies. Concobar, too, and all the Red Branch, rebuked the prophet. Yet he stood against them like a rock warred on by winds which stand immovable, let them rage as they will, and refused to take back his words. Then said Concobar:

"Many are the prophecies which came wandering down upon the mouths of men, but they are not all to be trusted alike. Of those which have passed thy lips, O Cathvah, we utterly reject the last, and think the less of thee for having reported it. But the former which concerns the child of promise hath been ever held a sure prophecy, and as such passed down through all the diviners from the time of Amargin, the son of Milesius, who first prophesied for the Gael. And now being arch-king of the Ultonians, I command thee to divine for us when the coming of the child shall be."

Then Cathvah, the Ard-Druid, put on his divining apparel and took his divining instruments in his hands, and made his symbols of power upon the air. And at first he was silent, and, being in a trance, stared out before him with wide eyes full of wonder and amazement, directing his gaze to the east. In the end he cried out with a loud voice, and prophesying, sang this lay:

"Yea, he is coming. He draweth nigh.
Verily It is he whom I behold -
The predicted one - the child of many prophecies -
Chief flower of the Branch that is over all -
The mainstay of Emaiti Macha - the battle-prop of
   the Ultonians -
The torch of the valour and chivalry of the North -
The star that is to shine for ever upon the forehead

of the Gael.
It is he who slumbers upon Slieve Fuad -
The child who is like a star -
Like a star upon Slieve Fuad.
There is a light around him never kindled at the
  hearth of Lu,
The Grey of Macha keeps watch and ward for him,

> [Footnote: Madia's celebrated grey war-steed.
> The meaning of the allusion will be understood
> presently.]

And the whole mountain is filled with the Tuatha de
Danan."

> [Footnote: These were the gods of the pagan
> Irish. Tuatha=nations, De=gods, Danan=of Dana.
> So it means the god nations sprung from Dana
> also called Ana. She is referred to in an ancient
> Irish Dictionary as Mater deorurn Hibern-
> ensium.]

Then his vision passed from the Druid, he raised up his
long white hands and gave thanks to the high gods of
Erin that he had lived to see this day.

When Cathvah had made an end of speaking there was
a great silence in the hall.

CHAPTER II

THE BOYS OF THE ULTONIANS

"And dear the school-boy spot
We ne'er forget though there we are forgot."

BYRON.

"There were his young barbarians all at play."

BYRON.

In the morning Fergus Mac Roy said to the young king, "What shall we do this day, O Concobar? Shall we lead forth our sweet-voiced hounds into the woods and rouse the wild boar from his lair, and chase the swift deer, or shall we drive afar in our chariots and visit one of our subject kings and take his tribute as hospitality, which, according to thee, wise youth, is the best, for it is agreeable to ourselves and not displeasing to the man that is tributary."

"Nay," said Concobar, "let us wait and watch this day. Hast thou forgotten the words of Cathvah?"

"Truly, in a manner I had," said Fergus, "for I never

Standish O'Grady

much regarded, the race of seers, or deemed the birds more than pleasant songsters, and the stars as a fair spectacle, or druidic instruments aught but toys."

"Let us play at chess on the lawn of the dun," said the king, "while our boys exercise themselves at hurling on the green."

"It is agreeable to me," said Fergus, "though well thou knowest, dear foster-son, that I am not thy match at the game."

What the champion said was true, for in royal wisdom the king far excelled his foster-father, and that was the reason why Fergus had abdicated the supreme captain-ship of the Red Branch in favour of Concobar, for though his heart was great his understanding was not fine and acute like the understanding of his foster-son.

The table was set for them upon the lawn before the great painted and glowing palace, and three-footed stools were put on either side of that table, and bright cloths flung over them. A knight to whom that was a duty brought forth and unfolded a chess-board of ivory on which silver squares alternated with gold, cunningly wrought by some ancient cerd, [Footnote: Craftsman.] a chief jewel of the realm; another bore in his hand the man-bag, also a wonder, glistening, made of netted wires of findruiney, [Footnote: A bright yellow bronze, the secret of making which is now lost. The metal may be seen in our museums. In beauty it is superior to gold.] and took therefrom the men and disposed them in their respective places on the board, each in the centre of his own square. The gold men were on the squares of silver, and the silver on the squares of gold. The table was set under the shadowing branches of a great tree, for it was early summer and the sun shone in his strength. So Concobar and Fergus, lightly laughing, affectionate and mirthful, the challenger and the challenged, came forth through the wide doorway of the dun. Armed youths went with them. The right arm of Fergus was cast lightly over the shoulder of Concobar, and his ear was inclined to him as the young king talked, for their mutual affection was very great and like that of a great boy and a small boy when such, as often happens, become attached to one another. So Concobar and Fergus sat down to play, though right seldom did the Champion win any game from the King. Concobar beckoned to him one of the young knights. It was Conall Carna, [Footnote: Conall the Victorious. He came second to Cuculain amongst the Red Branch Knights. He is the theme of many heroic stories. Once in a duel he broke the right arm of his opponent. He bade his seconds tie up his own corresponding arm.] son of Amargin, youngest of the knights of Concobar. "Son of Amargin," said the king, "do thou watch over the boys this day in their pastimes. See that nothing is done unseemly or unjust. Observe narrowly the behaviour and disposition of the lads, and report all things clearly to me on the morrow."

So saying, he moved one of the pieces on the board, and Conall Carna strode away southwards to where the boys were already dividing themselves into two parties for a match at hurling.

That son of Amargin was the handsomest youth of all the province. White and ruddy was his beardless countenance. Bright as gold which boils over the edge of the refiner's crucible was his hair, which fell curling upon his broad shoulders and over the circumference of his shield, outshining its splendour. By his side hung a short sword with a handle of walrus-tooth; in his left hand he bore two spears tipped with glittering bronze. Fergus and Concobar watched him as he strode over the grass; Concobar noted his beauty and grace, but Fergus noted his great strength. Soon the boys, being divided into two equal bands, began their pastime and contended, eagerly urging the ball to and fro. The noise of the stricken ball and the clash of the hurles shod with bronze, the cries of the captains, and the shouting of the boys, filled all the air.

That good knight stood midway between the goals, eastward from the players. Ever and anon with a loud clear voice he reproved the youths, and they hearkening took his rebukes in silence and obeyed his words. Cathvah came forth that day upon the lawn, and thus spoke one of the boys to another in some pause of the game, "Yonder, see! the Ard-Druid of the Province. Wherefore comes he forth from his druidic chambers to-day at this hour, such not being his wont?" And the other answered lightly, laughing, and with boyish heedlessness, "I know not wherefore; but well he knows himself." And therewith ran to meet the ball which passed that way. There was yet a third who watched the boys. He stood afar off on the edge of the plain. He had a little shield strapped on his back, two javelins in one hand, and a hurle in the other. He was very young and fair. He stood looking fixedly at the hurlers, and as he looked he wept. It was the child who had been promised to the Ultonians.

CHAPTER III

DETHCAEN'S NURSLING

"Very small and beautiful like a star."

HOMER.

"I love all that thou lovest,
Spirit of delight;
The fresh earth in new leaves drest,
And the blessed night;
Starry evening and the morn,
When the golden mists are born."

SHELLEY.

Sualtam of Dun Dalgan on the Eastern Sea, took to wife Dectera, daughter of Factna the Righteous. She was sister of Concobar Mac Nessa. Sualtam was the King of Cooalney [Footnote: Now the barony of Cooley, a mountainous promontory which the County of Louth projects into the Irish Sea.] a land of woods and mountains, an unproductive headland reaching out into the Ictian Sea.

Dectera bare a son to Sualtam, and they called him

Setanta, That was his first name. His nurse was Dethcaen, the druidess, daughter of Cathvah the druid, the mighty wizard and prophet of the Crave Rue. His breast-plate [Footnote: A poetic spell or incantation. So even the Christian hymn of St. Patrick was called the lorica or breastplate of Patrick.] of power, woven of druidic verse, was upon Ulla [Footnote: Ulla is the Gaelic root of Ulster.] in his time, upon all the children of Rury in their going out and their coming in, in war and in peace. Dethcaen [Footnote: Dethcaen is compounded of two words which mean respectively, colour, and slender.] sang her own songs of protection for the child. His mother gave the child suck, but the rosy-cheeked, beautiful, sweetly-speaking daughter of Cathvah nursed him. On her breast and knee she bare him with great love. Light of foot and slender was Dethcaen; through the wide dun of Sualtam she went with her nursling, singing songs. She it was that discovered his first ges, [Footnote: Ges was the Irish equivalent of the tabu.] namely, that no one should awake him while he slept. He had others, sacred prohibitions which it was unlawful to transgress, but this was discovered by Dethcaen. She discovered it while he was yet a babe. With her own hands Dethcaen washed his garments and bathed his tiny limbs; lightly and cheerfully she sprang from her couch at night when she heard his voice, and raised him from the cradle and wrapped him tenderly, and put him into the hands of his mother. She watched him when he slumbered; there was great stillness in the palace of Sualtam when the child slept. She repeated for him many tales and taught him nothing base. When he was three years old, men came with hounds to hunt the stream which ran past Dun Dalgan. [Footnote: Now Dundalk, capital of the County of Louth.] Early in the morning Setanta heard the baying of the hounds and the shouting of the men. They were hunting a great water-dog which had his abode in this stream. Setanta leaped from his couch and ran to the river. Well he knew that stream and all its pools and shallows; he knew where the water-dog had his den. Thither by circuit he ran and stood before the month of the same, having a stone in either hand. The hunted water-dog drew nigh. Maddened with fear and rage he gnashed his teeth and growled, and then charged at the child. There, O Setanta, with the stroke of one stone thou didst slay the water-dog! The dog was carried in procession with songs to the dun of Sualtam, who that night gave a great feast and called many to rejoice with him, because his only son had done bravely. A prophet who was there said, "Thou shalt do many feats in thy time, O Setanta, and the last will resemble the first."

Setanta played along the sand and by the frothing waves of the sea-shore under the dun. He had a ball and an ashen hurle shod with bronze; joyfully he used to drive his ball along the hard sand, shouting among his small playmates. The captain of the guard gave him a sheaf of toy javelins and taught him how to cast, and made for him a sword of lath and a painted shield. They made for him a high chair. In the great hall of the dun, when supper was served, he used to sit beside the champion of that small realm, at the south end of the table over against the king. Ever as evening drew on and the candles were lit, and the instruments of festivity and the armour and trophies on the walls and pillars shone in the cheerful light, and the people of Sualtam sat down rejoicing, there too duly appeared Setanta over against his father by the side of the champion, very fair and pure, yellow-haired, in his scarlet bratta fastened with a little brooch of silver, serene and grave beyond his years, shining there like a very bright star on the edge of a thunder-cloud, so that men often smiled to see them together.

While Sualtam and his people feasted, the harper harped and trained singers sang. Every day the floor was strewn with fresh rushes or dried moss or leaves. Every night at a certain hour the bed-makers went round spreading couches for the people of Sualtam. Sometimes the king slept with his people in the great hall. Then one warrior sat awake through the night at his pillow having his sword drawn, and another warrior sat at his feet having his sword drawn. The fire-place was in the midst of the hall. In winter a slave appointed for that purpose from time to time during the night laid on fresh logs. Rude plenty never failed in the dun of Sualtam. In such wise were royal households ordered in the age of the heroes. For the palace, it was of timber staunched with clay and was roofed with rushes. Without it was white with lime, conspicuous afar to mariners sailing in the Muirnict. [Footnote: The Irish Sea or St. George's Channel. Muirnict means the Ictian Sea.] There was a rampart round the dun and a moat spanned by a drawbridge. Before it there was a spacious lawn. Down that lawn there ever ran a stream of sparkling water. Setanta sailed his boats in the stream and taught it here to be silent, and there to hum in rapids, or to apparel itself in silver and sing liquid notes, or to blow its little trumpet from small cataracts.

CHAPTER IV

SETANTA RUNS AWAY

"For a boy's way is the wind's way."

LONGFELLOW

And now the daily life of that remote dun no longer pleased the boy, for the war-spirit within drave him on. Moreover he longed for comrades and playfellows, for his fearful mother permitted him no longer to associate with children of that rude realm whose conversation and behaviour she misliked for her child. She loved him greatly and perceived not how he changed, or how the new years in their coming and their going both gave and took away continually.

In summer the boy sat often with the chief bard under the thatched eaves of the dun, while the crying swallows above came and went, asking many questions concerning his forefathers back the ascending line up to Rury, and again downwards through the ramifications of that mighty stem, and concerning famous marches and forays, and battles and single combats, and who was worthy and lived and died well, and who not. More than all else he delighted to hear about Fergus Mac Roy, who seemed to him the greatest and best of all the Red Branch. In winter, cradled in strong arms, he listened to the reminiscences and conversation of the men of war as they sat and talked round the blazing logs in the hall, while the light flickered upon warlike faces, and those who drew drink went round bearing mead and ale.

Upon his seventh birthday early in the morning he ran to his mother and cried, "Mother, send me now to Emain Macha, to my uncle."

Dectera grew pale when she heard that word and her knees smote together with loving fear. For answer she withdrew him from the society of the men and kept him by herself in the women's quarter, which was called grianan. The grianan was in the north end of the palace behind the king's throne. In the hall men could see above them the rafters which upheld the roof and the joining of the great central pillar with the same. From the upper storey of the grianan a door opened upon the great hall directly above the throne of the king, and before that door was a railed gallery.

Thence it was the custom of Dectera to supervise in the morning the labours of the household thralls and at night to rebuke unseemly revelry, and at the fit hour to command silence and sleep. Thence too in the evening, ere he went to his small couch, Setanta would cry out "good-night" and "good slumber" to his friends in the hall, who laughed much amongst themselves for the secret of his immurement was not hid. Moreover, Dectera gave straight commandment to her women, at peril of her displeasure and of sore bodily chastisement, that they should not speak to him any word concerning Emain Macha. The boy as yet knew not where lay the wondrous city, whether in heaven or on earth or beyond the sea. To him it was still as it were a fairy city or in the land of dreams.

One day he saw afar upon the plain long lines of lowing kine and of laden garrans wending north-westward. He questioned his mother concerning that sight. She answered, "It is the high King's tribute out of Murthemney." [Footnote: A territory conterminous with the modern County of Louth.]

"Mother," he said, "how runs the road hence to the great city?"

"That thou shalt not know," said his mother, looking narrowly on the boy.

But still the strong spirit from within, irresistible, urged on the lad. One day while his mother conversed with him, inadvertently she uttered certain words, and he knew that the road to Emain Macha went past the mountain of Slieve Fuad. [Footnote: Now the Fews mountain lying on the direct way between Dundalk and Armagh.] That night he dreamed of Emain Macha, and he rose up early in the morning and clambered on to the roof of the palace through a window and gazed long upon the mountain. The next night too he dreamed of Emain Macha, and heard voices which were unintelligible, and again the third night he heard the voices and one voice said, "This our labour is vain, let him alone. He is some changeling and not of the blood of Rury. He will be a grazier, I think, and buy cattle and sell them for a profit." And the other said, "Nay, let us not leave him yet. Remember how valiantly he faced the fierce water-dog and slew him at one cast."

Standish O'Grady

When he climbed to the roof, as his manner was, to gaze at the mountain, he thought that Slieve Fuad nodded to him and beckoned. He broke fast with his mother and the women that day and ate and drank silently with bright eyes, and when that meal was ended he donned his best attire and took his toy weapons and a new ball and his ashen hurle shod with red bronze.

"Wherefore this holiday attire?" said his mother.

"Because I shall see great people ere I put it off," he answered.

She kissed him and he went forth as at other times to play upon the lawn by himself. The king sat upon a stone seat hard by the door of the grianan. Under the eaves he sat sunning himself and gazing upon the sea. The boy kneeled and kissed his hand. His father stroked his head and said, "Win victory and blessings, dear Setanta." He looked at the lad as if he would speak further, but restrained himself and leaned back again in his seat.

Dectera sat in the window of the upper chamber amongst her women. They sat around her sewing and embroidering. She herself was embroidering a new mantle for the boy against his next birthday, though that indeed was far away, but ever while her hands wrought her eyes were on the lawn.

"Mother," cried Setanta," watch this stroke."

He flung his ball into the air and as it fell met it with his hurle, leaning back and putting his whole force into the blow, and struck it into the clouds. It was long before the ball fell. It fell at his feet.

"Mother," he cried again, "watch this stroke."

He went to the east mearing of the spacious lawn and struck the ball to the west. It traversed the great lawn ere it touched the earth and bounded shining above the trees. Truly it was a marvellous stroke for one so young. As he went for his ball the boy stood still before the window. "Give me thy blessing, dear mother," he said.

"Win victory and blessing for ever, O Setanta," she answered. "Truly thou art an expert hurler."

"These feats," he replied, "are nothing to what I shall yet do in needlework, O mother, when I am of age to be trusted with my first needle, and knighted by thy hands, and enrolled amongst the valiant company of thy sewing-women."

"What meaneth the boy?" said his mother, for she perceived that he spoke awry.

"That his childhood is over, O Dectera," answered one of her women, "and that thou art living in the past and in dreams. For who can hold back Time in his career?"

The queen's heart leaped when she heard that word, and the blood forsook her face. She bent down her head over her work and her tears fell. After a space she looked out again upon the lawn to see if the boy had returned, but he had not.

She bade her women go and fetch him, and afterwards the whole household. They called aloud, "Setanta,

Setanta," but there was no answer, only silence and the watching and mocking trees and a sound like low laughter in the leaves; for Setanta was far away.

The boy came out of that forest on the west side. Soon he struck the great road which from Ath-a-clia [Footnote: Ath-a-cliah, i.e., the Ford of the Hurdles. It was the Irish name for Dublin.] ran through Murthemney to Emain Macha, and saw before him the purple mountain of Slieve Fuad. In his left hand was his sheaf of toy javelins; in his right the hurle; his little shield was strapped upon his back. The boy went swiftly, for there was power upon him that day, and with his ashen hurle shod with red bronze ever urged his ball forward. So he went driving, his ball before him. At other times he would cast a javelin far out westward and pursue its flight. Ever as he went there ever flew beside him a grey-necked crow. "It is a good omen," said the boy, for he knew that the bird was sacred to the Mor-Reega.

He was amazed at his own speed and the elasticity of his limbs. Once when he rose after having gathered his thrown javelin, a man stood beside him who had the port and countenance of some ancient hero, and whose attire was strange. He was taller and nobler than any living man. He bore a rod-sling in his right hand, and in his left, in a leash of bronze, he led a hound. The hound was like white fire. Setanta could hardly look in that man's face, but he did. The man smiled and said -

"Whither away, my son?"

"To Emain Macha, to my uncle Concobar," said the boy.

"Dost thou know me, Setanta?" said the man.

"I think thou art Lu Lam-fada Mac Ethlend," [Footnote: Lu the Long-Handed son of Ethlenn. This mysterious being, being one of the deities of the pagan Irish, seems to have been the Sun-god.] answered Setanta.

"I am thy friend," said the man, "fear nothing, for I shall be with thee always."

Then the man and the hound disappeared as if they had been resolved into the rays of the sun; Setanta saw nothing, only the grey-necked crow starting for flight. Then a second man in a wide blue mantle specked with white like flying foam came against him and flung his mantle over Setanta. There was a sound in his ears like the roaring of the sea. [Footnote: This man was Mananan son of Lir. He was the Sea-god.] Chariots and horses came from the east after that. Setanta recognised those who urged on the steeds, they were his own people. "Surely," he said, "I shall be taken now." The men drave past him. "If I mistake not," he said, "the man who flung his mantle over me was Mananan the son of Lir."

Divers persons, noble and ignoble, passed him on the way, some riding in chariots, some going on foot. They went as though they saw him not.

In the evening he came to Slieve Fuad. He gathered a bed of dried moss and heaped moss upon his shield for a pillow. He wrapped himself in his mantle, and lay down to sleep, and felt neither cold nor hunger. While he slept a great steed, a stallion, grey to whiteness, came close to him, and walked all round him, and smelt him, and stayed by him till the morning.

Setanta was awaked by the loud singing of the birds. Light of heart the boy started from his mossy couch and wondered at that tuneful chorus. The dawning day trembled through the trees still half-bare, for it was the month of May.

"Horses have been here in the night," said the boy, "one horse. What mighty hoof marks!" He wondered the more seeing how the marks encircled him. "I too will one day have a chariot and horses, and a deft charioteer." He stood musing, "Is it the grey of Macha? [Footnote: The goddess Macha, already referred to, had a horse which was called the Grey of Macha - Liath-Macha. He was said to be still alive dwelling invisibly in Erin.] They say that he haunts this mountain." He hastened to the brook, and finding a deep pool, bathed in the clear pure water and dried himself in his woollen bratta [Footnote: The Gaelic word for mantle.] of divers colours. Very happy and joyous was Setanta that day. And he spread out the bratta to dry, and put on his shirt of fine linen and his woollen tunic that reached to the knees in many plaits. Shoes he had none; bare and naked were his swift feet.

"This is the mountain of Fuad the son of Brogan," [Footnote: An ancient Milesian hero. Brogan was uncle of Milesius.] said he. "I would I knew where lies his cairn in this great forest that I might pay my stone-tribute to the hero." Soon he found it and laid his stone upon the heap. He climbed to the hill's brow and looked westward and saw far away the white shining duns of the marvellous city from which, even now, the morning smoke went up into the windless air. He trembled, and rejoiced, and wept. He stood a long time there gazing at Emain Macha. Descending, he struck again the great road, but he went slowly; he cast not his javelins and drave not his ball. Again, from a rising ground he saw Emain Macha, this time near at hand. He remained there a long time filled with awe and fear. He covered his head with his mantle and wept aloud, and said he would return to Dun Dalgan, that he dared not set unworthy feet in that holy place.

Then he heard the cheerful voices of the boys as they brake from the royal palace and ran down the wide smooth lawn to the hurling-ground. His heart yearned for their companionship, yet he feared greatly, and his mind misgave him as to the manner in which they would receive him. He longed to go to them and say, "I am little Setanta, and my uncle is the king, and I would be your friend and playfellow." Hope and love and fear confused his mind. Yet it came to him that he was urged forwards, by whom he knew not. Reluctantly, with many pausings, he drew nigh to the players and stood solitary on the edge of the lawn southwards, for the company that held that barrier were the weaker. He hoped that some one would call to him and welcome him, but none called or welcomed. Silently the child wept, and the front of his mantle was steeped in his tears. Some looked at him, but with looks of cold surprise, as though they said, "Who is this stranger boy and what doth he here? Would that he took himself away out of this and went elsewhere." The boy thought that he would be welcomed and made much of because he was a king's son and nephew of the high King of Ulla, and on account of his skill in hurling, and because he himself longed so exceedingly for companions and comrades, and because there were within him such fountains of affection and loving kindness. And many a time happy visions had passed before his eyes awake or asleep of the meeting between himself and his future comrades, but the event itself when it happened was by no means what he had anticipated. For no one kissed him and bade him welcome or took him by the right hand and led him in, and no one seemed glad of his coming and he was here of no account at all. Bitter truly was thy weeping, dear Setanta.

CHAPTER V

THE NEW BOY

"I to surrender, to fling away this! So owned by God and Man! so witnessed to! I had rather be rolled into my grave and buried with infamy." - Battle-chaunt of a hero of the Saxons.

Once, struck sideways out of the press, the ball bounded into a clear space not far from Setanta. "Thou of the Javelins," cried the captain of the distressed party, "the ball is with thee." He roared mightily at Setanta. On a sudden Setanta, filled with all the glow and ardour of the mimic battle, cast his javelins to the ground, slipped the strap of his shield over his head, flung the shield beside his javelins on the grass and pursued the bounding ball. He out-ran the rest and took possession of the ball. Now to the right he urged it, now to the left. He played it deftly before every opponent who sought to check his career, and swiftly and cunningly carried it past each of these, and finally with a clear loud stroke sent it straight as a sling-bolt through the middle of the north goal. The boys of his adopted party shouted, and they praised his playing and that final victorious stroke. Setanta went back after that and stood by himself near the south goal. His face was flushed and his eyes sparkled, and he himself trembled with joy, yet was he not in the least exhausted or out of breath.

The captain of the northern company came down with his boys and all the boys who were chief in authority, and they surrounded Setanta and said, "Thou art here a stranger and on sufferance. We know thee not, but thou art a good hurler and not otherwise, as we think, unmeet to bear us company. Receive now our protection, and we will divide the sides again with a new division and continue the game, for thou art very swift and truly expert in the use of thy hurle."

The boys regulated all things according to the laws and customs of their elders. And everywhere it was the custom that the weak should accept the protection of the strong and submit themselves to their command. So slaves received masters, so runaways and fugitives got to themselves lords, and sheltered themselves under their protection and paid dues. Setanta's brow fell, and he answered, "Put not upon me, I pray you, these hard terms. I would be your friend and comrade, I cannot be your subject being what I am."

And they said, "Who art thou?"

And he answered, "I am the son of Dectera of Dun Dalgan, and nephew of the king."

Then the boy who was captain of the whole school, and the biggest and strongest, stood over him, and said -

"Thou, the king's nephew! the son of Sualtam and Dectera of Dun Dalgan! and comest hither without chariots and horsemen and a prince's retinue and guard. Nay, thou art a churl and a liar to boot, and hie thee hence now with wings at thy heels or verily with sore blows I shall beat thee off the lawn."

Thereat the blood forsook thy face, O Setanta, O peerless one, and thou stoodest like a still figure carved out of white marble, with the pallor of death in thy immortal face. But that other, indignant to see him stand as one both deaf and dumb, and mistaking his pallor for fear, raised his hurle and struck with all his might at the boy. Setanta sprang back avoiding the blow, and ere the other could recover himself, struck him back-handed over the right ear, whose knees were suddenly relaxed and the useless weapon shaken from his hands. Then some stood aside, but the rest ran upon Setanta to beat him off the lawn and struck at him all together, as well as they could, for their numbers impeded them, and fiercely the stranger defended himself, and many a shrewd stroke he delivered upon his enemies, for the slumbering war-spirit now, for the first time, had awaked in his gentle heart. Many times he was overborne and flung to the ground, but again he arose overthrowing others, never quitting hold of his hurle, and, whenever he got a free space, grasping that weapon like a war-mace in both hands, he struck down his foes. The skirts of his mantle were torn, only a rag remained round his shoulders, fastened by the brooch; he was covered with blood, his own and his enemies', and his eyes were like burning fire. Then Conall Carna being enraged ran towards the boys, meaning to rebuke their cowardice and with his strong hands hurl them asunder and save the stranger boy. There was not a knight in all Ireland those days who loved battle-fairness better than Conall Carna. Truly he was the pure-burning torch of the chivalry of the Ultonians in his time.

But as he ran one withheld him and a voice crying "Forbear" rang in his ears. Yet he saw no man. He stood still, being astonished, and became aware that this tumult was divinely guided, for as in a trance he saw and heard marvellous things. For the war-steeds of the Ultonians neighed loudly in their stables, and from the Tec Brac, the Speckled House of the Red Branch, rose a clangour of brass, the roar of the shield called Ocean, and the booming of the Gate-of-Battle, and the singing of swords long silent, and the brazen thunder of the revolution of wheels; and he saw strange forms and faces in the air, and the steady sun dancing in the heavens, and a man standing beside the stranger whose face was like the sun. The son of Amargin saw and heard all, for he was a seer and a prophet no less than a warrior. But meantime his battle-fury descended upon Setanta, his countenance was distraught and his strength was multiplied tenfold, and the steam of his war-madness rose above him. He staggered to no blow, but every boy whom he struck fell, and he charged this way and that, and wherever he went they opened before him. Then seeing how they closed in behind him and on each side, he beat his way back to the grassy rampart in which was the goal, and, facing his enemies, bade them come against him again in their troops, many against one. "You have offered me your protection," he said, "and I would not endure it, but now I swear to you by all my gods that you and I do not part this day till you have accepted my protection, or till I lie without life on this lawn a trophy of your prowess and a monument of the chivalry and hospitality of the Red Branch." Then a boy stood out from the rest. He was freckled, and with red hair, and his voice was loud and fierce.

"Thou   shalt   have   a   comrade   in   thy   battle henceforward," he said, "O brave stranger. On the banks of the Nemnich, [Footnote: Now the Nanny-Water, a beautiful stream running from Tara to the sea.] where it springs beneath my father's dun on the Hill of Gabra, nigh Tara, I met a prophetess; Acaill is her name, the wisest of all women; and I asked her who would be my life-friend. And she answered, 'I see him standing against a green wall at Emain Macha, at bay, with the blood and soil of battle upon him, and alone he gives challenge to a multitude. He is thy life-friend, O Laeg,' she said, 'and no man ever had a friend like him or will till the end of time.'"

So saying he ran to Setanta, and kneeling down he took him by his right hand, and said, "I am thy man from this day forward." And after that he arose and kissed him, and standing by his side cried, "O Cumascra Mend Macha, O stammering son of Concobar, if ever I was a shield to thee against thy mockers, come hither; and thou too come O Art Storm-Ear, and thou Art of the Shadow, and thou O Fionn of the Songs, and you O Ide and Sheeling, who were nursed at the same breast and knee with myself." So he summoned to him his friends, and they came to him, and there came to him, uninvited, the three sons of Fergus and others whose hearts were stirred with shame or ruth. Yet, indeed, they were few compared with the multitude of his enemies. Then for the first time the boy's soul was confused, and he cried aloud, and bowed his head between his hands, and the hot tears gushed forth like rain from his eyes, mingled with blood. Soon, hearing the loud mockery and derisive laughter of his enemies, he hardened his heart and went out against them with these his friends, and drove them over the whole course of the playing-ground, and, hard by the north goal, he brake the battle upon them and they fled. Of the fugitives some ran round the King and the Champion where they sat, but Setanta running straight sprang lightly over the chess table. Then Concobar, reaching forth his left hand, caught him by the wrist and brought him to a stand, panting and with dilated eyes.

"Why art thou so enraged?" said the King, "and why dost thou so maltreat my boys?"

It was a long time before the boy answered, so furiously burned the battle-fire within him, so that the King repeated his question more than once. At last he made answer -

"Because they have not treated me with the respect due a stranger."

"Who art thou thyself?" said the King.

"I am Setanta, son of Sualtam and of Dectera thy own sister, and it is not before my uncle's palace that I should be dishonoured."

Concobar smiled, for he was well pleased with the appearance and behaviour of the boy, but Fergus caught him up in his great arms and kissed him, and he said -

"Dost thou know me, O Setanta?"

"I think thou art Fergus Mac Roy," he answered.

"Wilt thou have me for thy tutor?" said Fergus.

"Right gladly," answered Setanta. "For in that hope too

I left Dun Dalgan, coming hither secretly without the knowledge of my parents."

This was the first martial exploit of Setanta, who is also called Cuculain, and the reward of this his first battle was that the boys at his uncle's school elected him to be for their captain, and one and all they put themselves under his protection. And a gentle captain made he when the war-spirit went out of him, and a good play-fellow and comrade was Setanta amongst his new friends.

That night Setanta and Laeg slept in the same bed of healing after the physicians had dressed their wounds; and they related many things to each other, and oft times they kissed one another with great affection, till sweet sleep made heavy their eyelids.

So, impelled by the unseen, Setanta came to Emain Macha without the knowledge of his parents, but in fulfilment of the law, for at a certain age all the boys of the Ultonians should come thither to associate there with their equals and superiors, and be instructed by appointed tutors in the heroic arts of war and the beautiful arts of peace. Concobar Mac Nessa was not only King of Ulster and captain of the Red Branch, but was also the head and chief of a great school. In this school the boys did not injure their eyesight and impair their health by poring over books; nor were compelled to learn what they could not understand; nor were instructed by persons whom they did not wish to resemble. They were taught to hurl spears at a mark; to train war-horses and guide war-chariots; to lay on with the sword and defend themselves with sword and shield; to cast the hand-stone of the warrior - a great art in those days; to run, to leap, and to swim; to rear tents of turf and branches swiftly, and to roof them with sedge and rushes; to speak appropriately with equals and superiors and inferiors, and to exhibit the beautiful practices of hospitality according to the rank of guests, whether kings, captains, warriors, bards or professional men, or unknown wayfarers; and to play at chess and draughts, which were the chief social pastimes of the age; and to drink and be merry in hall, but always without intoxication; and to respect their plighted word and be ever loyal to their captains; to reverence women, remembering always those who bore them and suckled when they were themselves helpless and of no account; to be kind to the feeble and unwarlike; and, in short, all that it became brave men to feel and to think and to do in war and in peace. Also there were those who taught them the history of their ancestors, the great names of the Clanna Rury, and to distinguish between those who had done well and those who had not done so well, and the few who had done ill. And these their several instructors appointed by Concobar Mac Nessa and the council of his wise men were famous captains of the Ultonians, and approved bards and historians. And over all the high king of Ulster, Concobar Mac Nessa, was chief and president, not in name only but in fact, being well aware of all the instructors and all the instructed, and who was doing well and exhibiting heroic traits, and who was doing ill, tending downwards to the vast and slavish multitude whose office was to labour and to serve and in no respect to bear rule, which is for ever the office of the multitude in whose souls no god has kindled the divine fire by which the lamp of the sun, and the candles of the stars, and the glory and prosperity of nations are sustained and fed. Such, and so supervised, was the Royal School of Emain Macha in the days when Concobar Mac Nessa was King, and when

Fergus Mac Roy Champion, and when the son of Sualtam, not yet known by his rightful name, was a pupil of the same and under tutors and governors like the rest, though his fond mother would have evaded the law, for she loved him dearly, and feared for him the rude companionship and the stern discipline, the early rising and the strong labours of the great school.

CHAPTER VI

THE SMITH'S SUPPER PARTY

"Bearing on shoulders immense
Atlantean the weight,
Well nigh not to be borne,
Of the too vast orb of her fate."

MATTHEW ARNOLD.

One day, in the forenoon, a man came to Emain Macha. He was grim and swarthy, with great hands and arms. He made no reverence to Concobar or to any of the Ultonians, but standing stark before them, spake thus, not fluently: - "My master, Culain, high smith of all Ulster, bids thee to supper this night, O Concobar; and he wills thee to know that because he has not wide territories, and flocks, and herds, and tribute-paying peoples, only the implements of his industry, his anvils and hammers and tongs, and the slender profits of his labour, he feareth to feast all the Red Branch, who are by report mighty to eat and to drink; he would not for all Ireland bring famine upon his own industrious youths, his journeymen and his apprentices. Come therefore with a choice selection of thy knights, choosing those who are not great eaters, and drinkers, and you shall all have a fair welcome, a goodly supper, and a proportionate quantity of drink." That speech was a cause of great mirth to the Ultonians; nevertheless they restrained their laughter, so that the grim ambassador, who seemed withal to be a very angry man, saw nothing but grave countenances. Concobar answered him courteously, saying that he accepted the invitation, and that he would be mindful of the smith's wishes. When the man departed the Red Branch gave a loose rein to their mirth, each man charging the other with being in especial the person whose presence would be a cause of sorrow to the smith.

Culain was a mighty craftsman in those days. It was he who used to make weapons, armour, and chariots for the Ultonians, and there was never in Ireland a better smith than he. In his huge and smoky dun the ringing of hammers and the husky roar of the bellows seldom ceased; even at night the red glare of his furnaces painted far and wide the barren moor where he dwelt. Herdsmen and shepherds who, in quest of estrays, found themselves unawares in this neighbourhood, fled away praying to their gods, and, as they ran, murmured incantations.

In the afternoon Concobar, having made as good a selection as he could of his chief men, set forth to go. As they passed through the lawn he saw Setanta playing with his comrades. He stopped for a while to look, and then called the lad, who came at once and stood erect and silent before the King. He was now full ten years of age, straight and well-made and with sinews as hard as tempered steel. When he saw the company looking at him, he blushed, and his blushing became him well.

"Culain the smith," said Concobar, "hath invited us to a

feast. If it is pleasing to thee, come too."

"It is pleasing indeed," replied the boy, for he ardently desired to see the famous artificer, his people, his furnaces, and his engines. "But let me first, I pray thee, see this our game brought to an end, for the boys await my return. After that I will follow quickly, nor can I lose my way upon the moor, for the road hence to the smith's dun is well trodden and scored with wheels, and the sky too at night is red above the city."

Concobar gave him permission, and Setanta hastened back to his playmates, who hailed him gladly in his returning, for they feared that the King might have taken him away from them.

The King and his great men went away eastward after that and they conversed eagerly by the way, talking sometimes of a certain recent great rebellion of the non-Irian kings of Ulla, [Footnote: The Ultonians were descended from Ir, son of Milesius.] and of each other's prowess and the prowess of the insurgents, and sometimes of the smith and his strange and unusual invitation.

"Say no word and do no thing," said Concobar, "at which even a very angry and suspicious man might take offence, for as to our host and his artificers, their ways are not like ours, or their thoughts like our thoughts, and they are a great and formidable people."

The Red Branch did not relish that speech, for they thought that under the measureless canopy of the sky there were no people great or formidable but themselves.

CHAPTER VII

SETANTA AND THE SMITH'S DOG

"How he fell
From heaven, they fabled, thrown by angry Jove
Sheer o'er the crystal battlements; from morn
To noon, from noon to dewy eve,
A Summer's day, he fell; and with the setting sun
Dropped from the zenith like a falling star,
On Lemnos."

MILTON.

When Culain saw far away the tall figures of the
Ultonians against the sunset, and the flashing of their
weapons and armour, he cried out with a loud voice to
his people to stop working and slack the furnaces and
make themselves ready to receive the Red Branch; and
he bade the household thralls prepare the supper, roast,
boiled and stewed, which he had previously ordered.
Then he himself and his journeymen and apprentices
stripped themselves, and in huge keeves of water filled
by their slaves they washed from them the smoke and
sweat of their labour and put on clean clothes. The
mirrors at which they dressed themselves were the
darkened waters of their enormous tubs.

Culain sent a party of his men and those who were the best dressed and the most comely and who were the boldest and most eloquent in the presence of strangers, to meet the high King of the Ultonians on the moor, but he himself stood huge in the great doorway just beyond the threshold and in front of the bridge over which the Red Branch party was to pass. He had on him over his clothes a clean leathern apron which was not singed or scored. It was fastened at his shoulders and half covered his enormous hairy chest, was girt again at his waist and descended below his knees. He stood with one knee crooked, leaning upon a long ash-handled sledge with a head of glittering bronze. There he gave a friendly and grave welcome to the King and to all the knights one by one. It was dusk when Concobar entered the dun.

"Are all thy people arrived?" said the smith.

"They are," said Concobar.

Culain bade his people raise the drawbridge which spanned the deep black moat surrounding the city, and after that, with his own hands he unchained his one dog. The dog was of great size and fierceness. It was supposed that there was no man in Ireland whom he could not drag down. He had no other good quality than that he was faithful to his master and guarded his property vigilantly at night. He was quick of sight and hearing and only slept in the daytime. Being let loose he sprang over the moat and three times careered round the city, baying fearfully. Then he stood stiffly on the edge of the moat to watch and listen, and growled at intervals when he heard some noise far away. It was then precisely that Setanta set forth from Emain Macha. Earth quaked to the growling of that ill beast.

In the meantime the smith went into the dun, and when he had commanded his people to light the candles throughout the chamber, he slammed to the vast folding doors with his right hand and his left, and drew forth the massy bar from its place and shot it into the opposing cavity. There was not a knight amongst the Red Branch who could shut one of those doors, using both hands and his whole strength. Of the younger knights, some started to their feet and laid their hands on their sword hilts when they heard the bolt shot.

The smith sat down on his high seat over against Concobar, with his dusky sons and kinsmen around him, and truly they contrasted strangely with the bravery and beauty of the Ultonians. He called for ale, and holding in his hands a huge four-cornered mether of the same, rimmed with silver and furnished with a double silver hand-grip, he pledged the King and bade him and his a kindly welcome. He swore, too, that no generation of the children of Rury, and he had wrought for many, had done more credit to his workmanship than themselves, nor had he ever made the appliances of war for any of the Gael with equal pleasure. Concobar, on the other hand, responded discreetly, and praised the smith-work of Culain, praising chiefly the shield called Ocean [Footnote: Concobar's shield. When Concobar was in danger the shield roared. The sea, too, roared responsive.], which was one of the wonders of the north-west of Europe. The smith and all his people were well pleased at that speech, and Culain bade his thralls serve supper, which proved to be a very noble repast. There was enough and to spare for all the Ultonians. When supper was ended, the heroes and the artificers pledged each other many times and drank also to the memory of famous men of yore and their fathers who begat them, as was right and customary; and they became very friendly and merry without intoxication, for intoxication was not known in the age of the heroes.

Then said Concobar: "We have this night toasted many heroes who are gone, and, as it is not right that we should praise ourselves, I propose that we drink now to the heroes that are coming, both those unborn, and those who, still being boys, are under tutors and instructors; and for this toast I name the name of my nephew Setanta, son of Sualtam, who, if any, will one day, O Culain, if I mistake not, illustrate in an unexampled manner thy skill as an artificer of weapons and armour."

"Is he then a boy of that promise, O Concobar?" said the smith, "for if he is I am truly rejoiced to hear it."

"He is all that I say," answered the King somewhat hotly, "and of a beauty corresponding. And of that thou shalt be the judge to-night, for he is coming, and indeed I am momentarily expecting to hear the loud clamour of his brazen hurle upon the doors of the dun, after his having leapt at one bound both thy moat and thy rampart."

The smith started from his high seat uttering a great oath, such as men used then, and sternly chid Concobar because he had said that all his people had arrived. "If the boy comes now," he said, "ere I can chain the dog, verily he will be torn into small pieces."

Just then they heard the baying of the dog sounding terribly in the hollow night, and every face was blanched throughout the vast chamber. Then without was heard a noise of trampling feet and short furious yells and sibilant gaspings, as of one who exerts all his strength, after which a dull sound at which the earth seemed to shake, mingled with a noise of breaking bones, and after that silence. Ere the people in the dun could do more than look at each other speechless, they heard a clear but not clamorous knocking at the doors of the dun. Some of the smith's young men back-shot the bolt and opened the doors, and the boy Setanta stepped in out of the night. He was very pale. His scarlet mantle was in rags and trailing, and his linen tunic beneath and his white knees red with blood, which ran down his legs and over his bare feet. He made a reverence, as he had been taught, to the man of the house and to his people, and went backwards to the upper end of the chamber. The Ultonians ran to meet him, but Fergus Mac Roy was the first, and he took Setanta upon his mighty shoulder and bore him along and set him down at the table between himself and the King.

"Did the dog come against thee?" said Culain.

"Truly he came against me," answered the boy.

"And art thou hurt?" cried the smith.

"No, indeed," answered Setanta, "but I think he is."

At that moment a party of the smith's people entered the dun bearing between them the carcass of the dog from whose mouth and white crooked fangs the blood was gushing in red torrents; and they showed Culain how the skull of the dog and his ribs had been broken in pieces by some mighty blow, and his backbone also in divers places. Also they said: "One of the great brazen pillars which stand at the bridge head is bent awry, and the clean bronze denied with blood, and it was at the foot of that pillar we found the dog." So saying, they laid the body upon the heather in front of Culain's high seat, that it might be full in his eye, and when they did so and again sat down, there was a great silence in the chamber.

CHAPTER VIII

SETANTA, THE PEACE-MAKER

"The swine-herd of Bove Derg, son of the Dagda,

[Footnote: One of the minor gods. He resembles Mars Sylvanus of the Romans to whom swine were sacrificed.]

The feasts to which he came used to end in blood."

GAELIC BARD.

Culain sat silent for a long time looking out before him with eyes like iron, and when at last he spoke his voice was charged with wrath and sorrow.

"O Concobar," he said, "and you, the rest, nobles of the children of Rury. You are my guests to-night, wherefore it is not lawful that I should take vengeance upon you for the killing of my brave and faithful hound, who was a better keeper of my treasures than a company of hired warriors. Truly he cost me nothing but his daily allowance of meat, and there was not his equal as a watcher and warder in the world. An eric, therefore, I must have. Consult now together concerning its amount and let the eric be great and conspicuous, for, by Orchil [Footnote: The queen of the infernal regions.] and all the gods who rule beneath the earth, a small eric I will not accept."

Concobar answered straight, "Thou shalt not get from me or from the Ultonians any eric, small or great. My nephew slew the beast in fair fight, defending his life against an aggressor. But I will say something else, proud smith, and little it recks me whether it is pleasing to thee or not. Had thy wolf slain my nephew not one of you would have left this dun alive, and of your famous city of artificers I would have made a smoking heap."

The Ultonians fiercely applauded that speech, declaring that the smiths should get no eric, great or small, for the death of their monster. The smiths thereupon armed themselves with their hammers, and tongs, and fire-poles, and great bars of unwrought brass, and Culain himself seized an anvil withal to lay waste the ranks of the Red Branch. The Ultonians on their side ran to the walls and plucked down their spears from the pegs, and they raised their shields and balanced their long spears, and swords flashed and screeched as they rushed to light out of the scabbards, and the vast chamber glittered with shaking bronze and shone with the eyeballs of angry men, and rang with shouts of defiance and quick fierce words of command. For the Red Branch embattled themselves on one side of the chamber and the smiths upon the other, burning with unquenchable wrath, earth-born. The vast and high dome re-echoing rang with the clear terrible cries of the Ultonians and the roar of the children of the gloomy Orchil, and, far away, the magic shield moaned at Emain Macha, and the waves of the ocean sent forth a cry, for the peril of death and of shortness of life were around Concobar in that hour. And, though the doors of thick oak, brass-bound, were shut and barred, there came a man into the assembly, and he was not seen. He was red all over, both flesh and raiment, as if he had been plunged in a bath of blood. His countenance was distraught and his eyes like those of an insane man, and sparks new from them like sparks from a smith's stithy when he mightily hammers iron plucked white from the furnace. Smoke and fire came from his mouth. He held in his hand a long boar-yard. The likeness of a boar bounded after him. He traversed the vast chamber with the velocity of lightning, and with his boar-yard beat such as were not already drunk with wrath and battle-fury, and shot insane fire into their souls. [Footnote: This was the demon referred to in the lines at the head of the chapter.]

Then indeed it wanted little, not the space of time during which a man might count ten, for the beginning of a murder grim and great as any renowned in the world's chronicles, and it is the opinion of the learned that, in spite of all their valour and beautiful weapons, the artificers would then and there have made a bloody end of the Red Branch had the battle gone forward. But at this moment, ere the first missile was hurled on either side, the boy Setanta sprang into the midst, into the middle space which separated the enraged men, and cried aloud, with a clear high voice that rang distinct above the tumult -

"O Culain, forbear to hurl, and restrain thy people, and you the Ultonians, my kinsmen, delay to shoot. To thee, O chief smith, and thy great-hearted artificers I will myself pay no unworthy eric for the death of thy brave and faithful hound. For verily I will myself take thy dog's place, and nightly guard thy property, sleepless as he was, and I will continue to do so till a hound as trusty and valiant as the hound whom I slew is procured for thee to take his place, and to relieve me of that duty. Truly I slew not thy hound in any wantonness of superior strength, but only in the defence of my own life, which is not mine but my King's. Three times he leaped upon me with white fangs bared and eyes red with murder, and three times I cast him off, but when the fourth time he rushed upon me like a storm, and when with great difficulty I had balked him on that occasion also, then I took him by the throat and by his legs and flung him against one of the brazen pillars withal to make him stupid. And truly it was not my intention to kill him and I am sorry that he is dead, seeing that he was so faithful and so brave, and so dear to thee whom I have always honoured, even when I was a child at Dun Dalgan, and whom, with thy marvel-working craftsman, I have for a long time eagerly desired to see. And I thought that our meeting, whensoever it might be, would be other than this and more friendly."

As he went on speaking the fierce brows of the smith relaxed, and first he regarded the lad with pity, being so young and fair, and then with admiration for his bravery. Also he thought of his own boyish days, and as he did so a torrent of kindly affection and love poured from his breast towards the boy, yea, though he saw him standing before him with the blood of his faithful hound gilding his linen lena and his white limbs. Yet, indeed, it was not the hound's blood which was on the boy, but his own, so cruelly had the beast torn him with his long and strong and sharp claws.

"That proposal is pleasing to me," he said, "and I will

accept the eric, which is distinguished and conspicuous and worthy of my greatness and of my name and reputation amongst the Gael. Why should a man be angry for ever when he who did the wrong offers due reparation?" Therewith over his left shoulder he flung the mighty anvil into the dark end of the vast chamber among the furnaces, at the sound of whose falling the solid earth shook. On the other hand Concobar rejoiced at this happy termination of the quarrel, for well he knew the might of those huge children of the gloomy Orchil. He perceived, too, that he could with safety entrust the keeping of the lad to those people, for he saw the smith's countenance when it changed, and he knew that among those artificers there was no guile.

"It is pleasing to me, too," he said, "and I will be myself the lad's security for the performance of his promise."

"Nay, I want no security," answered the smith. "The word of a scion of the Red Branch is security enough for me."

Thereafter all laid aside their weapons and their wrath. The smiths with a mighty clattering cast their tools into the dark end of the chamber, and the Ultonians hanged theirs upon the walls, and the feasting and pledging and making of friendly speeches were resumed. There was no more any anger anywhere, but a more unobstructed flow of mutual good-will and regard, for the Ultonians felt no more a secret inclination to laugh at the dusky artificers, and the smiths no longer regarded with disdain the beauty, bravery, and splendour of the Ultonians.

In the meantime Setanta had returned to his place

between the King and Fergus Mac Roy. There a faintness came upon him, and a great horror overshadowed him owing to his battle with the dog, for indeed it was no common dog, and when he would have fallen, owing to the faintness, they pushed him behind them so that he lay at full length upon the couch unseen by the smiths. Concobar nodded to his chief Leech, and he came to him with his instruments and salves and washes. There unobserved he washed the cruel gashes cut by the hound's claws, and applied salves and stitched the skin over the wounds, and, as he did so, in a low voice he murmured healing songs of power.

"Where is the boy?" said Culain.

"He is reposing a little," said Concobar, "after his battle and his conflict."

After a space they gave Setanta a draught of mighty ale, and his heart revived in him and the colour returned to his cheeks wherein before was the pallor of death, and he sat up again in his place, slender and fair, between Concobar and Fergus Mac Roy. The smiths cried out a friendly welcome to him as he sat up, for they held him now to be their foster-son, and Culain himself stood up in his place holding in both hands a great mether [Footnote: A four-cornered quadrangular cup.] of ale, and he drank to all unborn and immature heroes, naming the name of Setanta, son of Sualtam, now his dear foster-son, and magnified his courage, so that the boy blushed vehemently and his eyelids trembled and drooped; and all the artificers stood up too and drank to their foster-son, wishing him victory and success, and they drained their goblets and dashed them, mouth downwards, upon the brazen tables, so that the clang reverberated over Ulla. Setanta thereupon stood up while the smiths roared a welcome to their foster-son, and he said that it was not he who had gained the victory, for that someone invisible had assisted him and had charged him with a strength not his own. Then he faltered in his speech and said again that he would be a faithful hound in the service of the artificers, and sat down. The smiths at that time would not have yielded him for all the hounds in the world.

After that their harpers harped for them and their story tellers related true stories, provoking laughter and weeping. There was no story told that was not true in the age of the heroes. Then the smiths sang one of their songs of labour, though it needed the accompaniment of ringing mettle, a song wild and strange, and the Ultonians clear and high sang all together with open mouths a song of battle and triumph and of the marching home to Emain Macha with victory; and so they spent the night, till Concobar said -

"O Culain, feasting and singing are good, but slumber is good also. Dismiss us now to our rest and our slumber, for we, the Red Branch, must rise betimes in the morning, having our own proper work to perform day by day in Emain Macha, as you yours in your industrious city."

With difficulty were the smiths persuaded to yield to that request, for right seldom was there a feast in Dun Culain, and the unusual pleasure and joyful sense of comradeship and social exaltation were very pleasing to their hearts.

The Ultonians slept that night in the smiths' hall upon resplendent couches which had been prepared for them, and early in the morning, having taken a friendly leave of the artificers, they departed, leaving the lad behind them asleep. Setanta remained with the smiths a long time after that, and Culain and his people loved him greatly and taught him many things. It was owing to this adventure and what came of it that Setanta got his second name, viz., the Hound of Culain or Cu-Culain. Under that name he wrought all his marvellous deeds.

CHAPTER IX

THE CHAMPION AND THE KING

"Sing, O Muse, the destructive wrath of Achilles, son of Peleus, which brought countless woes upon the Achaeans."

Homer.

Concobar Mac Nessa sat one day in his high chair, judging the Ultonians. His great Council sat before him. In the Champion's throne sat Fergus Mac Roy. Before the high King his suitors gave testimony and his brehons pleaded, and Concobar in each case pronounced judgment, clearly and intelligently, briefly and concisely, with learning and with equity.

"Right glad am I, O Concobar," said Fergus, "that thou art in the King's throne, and I where I sit. Verily, had I remained in that chair of honour and distress, long since would these historians and poets and subtle-minded lawyers have talked and rhymed me into madness, or into my grave."

Concobar made answer - "Dear foster-father, the high gods in their wisdom have fashioned us each man to illustrate some virtue. To thee they have given

Standish O'Grady

strength, courage, and magnanimity above all others; and to me, in small measure, the vision of justice, and the perception of her beautiful laws. A man can only excel in what he loves, and verily I love well the known laws of the Ultonians."

A great man just then entered the hall. His mantle was black. In the breast of it, instead of a brooch, he wore an iron pin. He came swiftly and without making the customary reverences. His face was pale, and his garments torn, his dark-grey tunic stained with blood. He stood in the midst and cried -

"O high King of the Ultonians, and you the wise men and sages of the children of Rury, to all of you there is now need of some prudent resolution. A great deed has been done in Ulla."

"What is that?" said the King.

"The abduction of the Beautiful Woman by Naysi, son of Usna. Verily, she is taken away and may not be recovered, for the Clan Usna came last night with a great company to the dun and they stormed it in their might and their valour, and their irresistible fury, and they have taken away Deirdre in their swift chariots, and have gone eastwards to the Muirnicht with intent to cross the sea northwards, and abide henceforth with their prize in the land of the Picts and of the Albanah, beyond the stormy currents of the Moyle."

Fergus Mac Roy, when he heard that word, sat up with eyes bright-blazing in his head. Dearer to him than all the rest were those sons of Usna, namely - Naysi, Anli, and Ardane, and dearest of the three was Naysi, who excelled all the youth of his time in beauty, valour, and accomplishments.

"Bind that man!" cried Concobar. His voice rang terribly through the vast chamber. Truly it sheared through men's souls like a dividing sword.

His guards took the man and bound him. "Lead him away now," said Concobar," and stone him with stones even to the parting of body with soul."

The man was one of Deirdre's guard.

A great silence fell upon the assembly after that and no man spoke, only they looked at the King and then again at the Champion, and, as it were, questioned one another silently with their eyes. It was the silence behind which run the Fomorh, brazen-throated and clad with storm. Well knew those wise men that what they long apprehended had come now to pass, namely, the fierce and truceless antagonism of the King and of the ex-King. Well they knew that Concobar would not forgive the Clan Usna, and that Fergus Mac Roy would not permit them to be punished. Therefore, great and mighty as were the men, yet on this occasion they might be likened only to cattle who stand aside astonished when two fierce bulls, rending the earth as they come, advance against each other for the mastery of the herd. In the high King's face the angry blood showed as two crimson spots one on either cheek, and his eyes, harder than steel, sparkled under brows more rigid than brass. On the other hand, the face of the Champion darkened as the sea darkens when a black squall descends suddenly upon its sunny and glittering tides, wrinkling and convulsing all the face of the deep. His listlessness and amiability alike went out of him, and he sat huge and erect in his throne. His mighty chest expanded and stood out like a shield, and the muscles of his neck, stronger than a bull's, became clear and distinct, and his gathering ire and stern resolution rushed stormfully through his nostrils. The King first spoke.

"To the man who has broken our law and abducted the child of ill omen, I decree death by the sword and burial with the three throws of dishonour, and if taken alive, then death by burning with the same, and if he escapes out of Erin, then sentence of perpetual banishment and expatriation."

"He shall not be slain, and he shall not be burned, and he shall not be exiled. I say it, even I, Fergus, son of the Red Rossa, Champion of the North. Let the man who will gainsay me show himself now in Emain Macha. Let him bring round the buckle of his belt."

His eyes, as he spoke, were like flames of fire under a forehead dark crimson, and with his clenched fist he struck the brazen table before his throne, so that the clang and roar of the quivering bronze sounded through all the borders of Ulla.

"I will gainsay thee, O Fergus," cried the King, "I am the guardian and the executor of the laws of the Ultonians, and those laws shall prevail over thee and over all men."

"All laws in restraint of true love and affection are unjust," said Fergus, "and the law by which Deirdre was consigned to virginity was the unrighteous enactment of cold-hearted and unrighteous men."

CHAPTER X

DEIRDRE

"Beautiful the beginning of love,
A man and a woman and the birds of Angus above
them."

GAELIC BARD.

The birth of the child Deirdre, daughter of the chief poet of Ulla, was attended with a great portent, for the child shrieked from the mother's womb. Cathvah and the Druids were consulted concerning that omen. They addressed themselves to their art of divination, and having consulted their oracles and gods and familiar spirits, they gave a clear counsel to the Ultonians.

"This child," they said, "will become a woman, in beauty surpassing all the women who have ever been born or will be born. Her union with a man will be a cause of great sorrow to the Ultonians. Let her, therefore, be exposed after birth; or, if you would not slay the Arch-Poet's only child, let her be sternly immured; let her be reared to womanhood in utter and complete and inviolable solitude, and live and die in her virginity."

The Ultonians determined that the child should live and be immured. These things took place in the reign of Factna the Righteous, father of Concobar. When the child was born she was called Deirdre. The Ultonians appointed for her a nurse and tutoress named Levarcam. They built for her and for the nurse a strong dun in a remote forest and set a ward there, and they made a solemn law enjoining perpetual virginity on the child of ill omen, and the Druids shed a zone of terror round the dun.

Concobar Mac Nessa in the wide circuit of his thoughts consulted always for the inviolability of that law, and the stern maintenance of the watching and warding.

Unseen and unobserved, forgotten by all save the wise elders of the Ultonians and by Concobar their King, whose thoughts ranged on all sides devising good for the Red Branch, the child Deirdre grew to be a maiden. Though her beauty was extraordinary, yet her mind was as beautiful as her form, so that the Lady Levarcam loved her exceedingly.

One day when the first flush of early womanhood came upon the maiden, she said to her tutoress as they sat together and conversed -

"Are all men like those our guards who defend us against savage beasts and the merciless Fomorians, dear Levarcam?"

"Those our guards are true and brave men," said Levarcam.

"Surely they are," said the girl, "and we lack no

courtesy and due attention at their hands, but dear foster-mother, my question is not answered. Maybe it is not to be answered and that I am curious overmuch. Are all men grim, grave, and austere, wearing rugged countenances scored with ancient wounds, and bearing each man upon his shoulders the weight of some fearful responsibility? Are all men like that, dear Levarcam?"

"Nay, indeed," said the other, "there arc youths too, gracious, and gay, and beautiful, as well as grave men such as these."

They sat together in their sunny grianan, [Footnote: A derivative from Grian, the sun. The grianan was an upper chamber, more elegantly furnished than the hall, usually with large windows and therefore well lit and reserved for the use of women.] embroidering while they conversed. It was early morning and the air was full of the noises and odours of sweet spring-time.

"I know that now," said the maiden, "which I only guessed before, for waking or sleeping I have dreamed of a youth who was as unlike these men as the rose-tree with its roses is unlike the rugged oak-tree or the wrinkled pine that has wrestled with a thousand storms. I would wish to have him for a playfellow and pleasant acquaintance. Of maidens, too, such as myself I have dreamed, yet they do not appear to me to be so alluring or so amiable as that youth."

"Describe him more particularly," said Levarcam. "Tell me his tokens one by one that I may know."

"He is tall and strong but very graceful in all his motions; and of speech and behaviour both gay and gracious. He is white and ruddy, whiter than snow and ruddier than the rose or the fox-glove, where the heroic blood burns bright in his comely cheeks. His eyes are blue-black under fine and even brows and his hair is a wonder, so dense is it, so lustrous and so curling, blacker than the crow's wing, more shining than the bright armour of the chaffer. His body is broad above and narrow below, strong to withstand and agile to pursue. His limbs long and beautifully proportioned; his hands and feet likewise, and his step elastic Smiles seldom leave his eyes and lips, and his mouth is a fountain of sweet speech. O that I were acquainted with him and he with me? I think we should be happy in each other's company. I think I could love him as well as I do thee, dear foster-mother."

As she spoke, Deirdre blushed, and first she stooped down over her work and then put before her face and eyes her two beautiful hands, rose-white, with long delicate nails pink-flushed and transparent; and tears, clearer than dewdrops, gushed between her ringers and fell in bright showers upon the embroidery. Then she arose and flung her soft white arms around Levarcam and wept on her bosom.

"There is one youth only amongst the Red Branch," said Levarcam, "who answers to that description, namely Naysi, the son of Usna, who is the battle-prop of the Ultonians and the clear-shining torch of their valour, and what god or druid or power hath set that vision before thy mind, I cannot tell."

"Would that I could see him with eyes and have speech with him," answered the girl. "If but once he smiled upon me and I heard the sweet words flow from his mouth which is beyond price, then gladly would I die!"

"Thou shall both see him and have speech with him, O best, sweetest, dearest, and loveliest of all maidens. Truly I will bring him to thee and thee to him, for there is with me power beyond the wont of women."

Now Levarcam was a mighty Druidess amongst the Ultonians. So the lady in whom they trusted forgot the ancient prophecies and the stern commands of the Red Branch and of their King, owing to the great love which she bore to the maiden and the great compassion which grew upon her day by day, as she observed the life of the solitary girl and thought of the cruel law to which all her youth and beauty and wealth of sweet love beyond all the jewels of the world were thus barbarously sacrificed by the Ultonians in obedience to soothsayers and Druids.

Naysi, son of Usna, once in a hunting became separated from his companions. He wandered far in that forest, seeking some one who should direct him upon his way. Oftentimes he raised his voice, but there was no answer. Such were his beauty, his grace, and his stature, that he seemed more like a god than a man, and such another as Angus Ogue, son of Dagda, [Footnote: Angus Ogue was the god of youth and beauty, son of the Dagda who seems to have been the genius of earth and its fertility or perhaps the Zeus of our Gaelic mythology.] whose fairy palace is on the margin of the Boyne. His head and his feet were bare. His short hunting-cloak was dark-red with flowery devices along the edge. On his breast he wore a brooch of gold bronze; carbuncles and precious stones were set in the bronze, and it was carved all over with many spiral devices. His shirt below the mantle was coloured like the tassels of the willow trees. His hair was fastened behind with a clasp and an apple of red gold, and that apple lay below the blades of his ample shoulders. In one hand he bore a broken leash of red bronze, and in the other two hunting spears with blades of flashing findruiney and the hafts were long, slender, and shining. By his thigh hung a short sword in a sheath of red yew and beside it the polished and nigh transparent horn of the Urus, suspended in a baldrick of knitted thread of bronze. The grass stood erect from the pressure of his light feet. His manly face had not yet known the razor; only the first soft down of budding manhood was seen there. His countenance was pure and joyous with bright beaming eyes, and his complexion red and white and of a brilliancy beyond words. In his heart was no guile, only indomitable valour and truth and loyalty and sweet affection. He had never known woman save in the way of courtesy. The very trees and rocks and stones seemed to watch him as he passed.

Then suddenly and unawares an ice-cold air struck chill into his inmost being, the bright earth was obscured and the sun grew dark in the heavens and menacing voices were heard and horrid forms of evil, monstrous, not to be described, came against him, and they bade him return as he had come or they would tear him limb from limb in that forest. Yet the son of Usna was by no means dismayed, only he flushed with wrath and scorn and he drew his sword and went on against the phantoms. In truth Naysi was at that moment passing through the zone of terror which the Ultonian Druids had shed around the dun where Deirdre was immured. The phantoms gave way before him and Naysi passed beyond the zone. "Surely," he said, "there is some chief jewel of the jewels of the world preserved in this place."

He came to an opening in the forest. Beyond it there was a great space which was cleared and girt all round by trees. There was a dun in its midst. Scarlet and white were the walls of that dun. There was a watch-tower on one side of the dun and a man there sitting in the watchman's seat; a grianan on the other with windows of glass. The roof of the dun was covered all over with feathers of birds of various hues, and shone with a hundred colours. The doorway was the narro-west which Naysi had ever seen. The door pillars were of red yew curiously carved, having feet of bronze and capitals of carved silver, and the lintel above was a straight bar of pure silver. A knotted band or thickening ran round the walls of the dun like a variegated zone, for the colours of it were many and each different from the colours on the walls. In the world there was no such prison as there was no such captive as that prison held. Armed men of huge stature and terrible aspect went round the dun. Their habiliments were black, their weapons without ornament, the pins of their mantles were of iron. With each company went a slinger having his sling bent, an iron bolt in the sling, and his thumb in the string-loop, men who never missed their mark and never struck aught, whether man or beast, that they did not slay. Great hounds such as were not known amongst the Ultonians went with those men. They were grey above and tawny beneath, as large as wild oxen after the growth of one year. They were quick of sight and scent, fiercer than dragons and swifter than eagles; they were not quick of sight and scent to-day. The Lady Levarcam had great power. In and around that dun were three hundred men of war, foreigners, picked men of the great fighting tribes of Banba. Such was the decree of the Ultonians and their wise King, so greatly did they fear concerning those prophecies and omens and concerning the child who in Emain Macha shrieked out of her mother's womb. Naysi regarded the dun with wonder and amazement, and with amazement the astonishing rigour of the watch and ward which were kept there, and the more he looked the more he wondered. It seemed to the hunter that he had chanced upon one of the abodes of the enchanted races of Erin, namely the Tuatha De Dana or the Fomorians, whom the sons of Milesius by their might had driven into the mountains and unfrequented places and who, now immortal and invisible, and possessing great druidic power, were worshipped as gods by the Gael. He knew he was in great peril, but his stout heart did not fail; he was resolved to see this adventure to an end.

As he was about to step out into the open two women came from the door of the grianan. One of them was old; she leaned upon her companion and in her right hand held a long white wand squared save in the middle where it was rounded for the hand grip, very long, unornamented, and unshod at either extremity. Naysi paid slight attention to her, though, as she was the first to come forth, he observed these things. The other was young, tall, slender, and lissom, her raiment costly and splendid like a high queen's on some solemn day, and like a queen's her behaviour and her pacing over the flowery lawn. Never had that hunter seen such a form, so proudly modest and virginal, such sweetness, grace, and majesty of bearing. Presently, having passed a company of the guards, she flung back the white, half-transparent veil that concealed her face. Then the sudden radiance was like the coming unlocked for out of a white cloud of that very bright star which shines on the edge of night and morning. All things were transfigured in her light. Before her the grass grew greener and more glittering and rare flowers started in her way. A silver basket of most delicate craftsmanship, the work of some cunning cerd, was on her right arm. It shone clear and sparkling against her mantle which was exceedingly lustrous, many times folded, darkly crimson, and of substance unknown. She towered above her aged companion, straight as a pillar of red yew in a king's house. So, unwitting, jocund, and innocent, fresh and pure as the morning, she paced over the green lawn, going in the direction of that youth, even Naysi, son of Usna the Ultonian. Naysi's loudly beating heart fell silent when he saw how she came straight towards him; he retreated into the forest, so amazing and so confounding was the radiance of that beauty. A company of those grim warders, silent and watchful, followed close upon the women. As they went they slipped the muzzles from the mouths of their dogs and lead them forward leashed. The countenances of the men shewed displeasure. From the tower the watchman cried aloud words in an unknown tongue, hoarse, barbaric accents charged with energy and strong meaning. His voice rang terribly in the hollows of the forest. There was a counter challenge in the forest repeated many times, the voices of men mingled with the baying of hounds. There was a ring of sentinels and dogs far out in the forest. The son of Usna had gone through the ring. For twice seven years and one that astonishing watch and ward had been maintained day and night without relaxation or abatement. When they came to the edge of the forest Levarcam addressed the commander of that company. She said, "The Lady Deirdre would be alone with me in the forest for a little space to gather flowers and listen to the music of the birds and the stream, relieved, if but for one moment, of this watching and warding."

Standish O'Grady

The man answered not a word. He was of the Gamanrdians, dwellers by the Sue, which feeds the great Western River; [Footnote: The Shannon.] his people were of the Clan Dega in the south, and of the children of Orc [Footnote: In scriptural language "of the seed of the giants," huge, simple-hearted and simple-minded men, who could obey orders and ask no questions.] from the Isles of Ore in the frozen seas. [Footnote: The Orkney Islands.] The blood of the Fomoroh was in those men. The women went on, and that grim company followed, keeping close behind. When they gained the first cover of the trees Levarcam turned round and stretched over them her wand. They stood motionless, both men and dogs. Then the women went forward, and alone.

"Fill thy basket now with forest flowers, O sweetest, and dearest, and fairest of all foster-children, and listen to the songs of the birds and the music of the rill. Cull thy flowers, darling girl, and cull the flower of thy youth, the flower that grows but once for all like thee, the flower whose glory puts high heaven to shame, and whose odour makes mad the most wise."

"Where shall I gather that flower, O gentlest and most amiable of foster-mothers? Is it in the glade or the thicket, or on the margent of the rill?

"It is not to be found by seeking, O fairest of all maidens. Gather it when thou meetest with it in the way. Wear it in thy heart, be the end what it may. Verily thou wilt not mistake any other flower for that flower."

"I know not thy meaning, O wise and many-counselled woman, but there is fear upon me, and trembling, and my knees quake at thy strange words. Now, if the whole world were swallowed up I should not be surprised. Surely the end of the world is very nigh."

"It is the end of the world and the beginning of the world; and the end of life and the beginning of life; and death and life in one, and death and life will soon be the same to thee, O Deirdre!"

"There is amazement upon me, and terror, O my foster-mother, on account of thy words, and on account of the gathering of this flower. Let us return to the dun. Terrible to me are the hollow-sounding ways of the unknown forest."

"Fear not the unknown forest, O Deirdre. Leave the known and the familiar now that thy time has come. Go on. Accomplish thy destiny. It is vain to strive against fate and the pre-ordained designs of the high gods of Erin. Truly I have failed in my trust. I see great wrath in Emain Macha. I see the Red Branch tossed in storms, and a mighty riving and rending and scattering abroad, and dismal conflagrations, and the blood of heroes falling like rain, and I hear the croaking of Byves. [Footnote: Badb, pronounced Byve, was primarily the scald-crow or carrion-crow, secondarily a Battle-Fury.] Truly I have proved a brittle prop to the Ultonians, but some power beyond my own drives me on."

"What wild words are these, O wisest of women, and what this rending and scattering abroad, and showers of blood and croaking of Byves because I cull a flower in the forest?"

"Nay, it is nothing. Have peace and joy while thou

canst, sweet Deirdre. Thus I lay my wand upon thy bosom and enjoin peace!"

"Thou art weary, dear foster-mother. Rest thee here now a little space, while I go and gather forest flowers. They are sweeter than those that grow in my garden. O, right glad am I to be alone in the forest, relieved from the observation of those grim-visaged sentinels, to stray solitary in the dim mysterious forest, and to think my own thoughts there, and dream my dreams, and recall that vision which I have seen. O Naysi, son of Usna, sweeter than harps is the mere sound of thy name, O Ultonian!"

Deirdre after that went forward alone into the forest.

Naysi, when he had started back into the forest stood still for a long time in his retreat. It was the hollow of a tall rock beside a falling stream of water, all flowing snow or transparent crystal. Holly trees and quicken trees grew from its crest, and long twines of ivy fell down before like green torrents. Behind them he concealed himself, when he heard the cries and the challengings and the baying of the hounds. Then he saw the maiden come along the forest glade by the margent of the stream, her basket filled and over-flowing with flowers. The sentient stream sang loud and gay to greet her approaching, with fluent liquid fingers striking more joyously the chords of his stony lyre. Light beyond the sun was shed through the glen before her. Birds, the brightest of plumage and sweetest of note of all the birds of Banba, [Footnote: One of Ireland's ancient names.] filled the air with their songs, flying behind her and before her, and on her right hand and on her left. Through his lattice of trailing ivy the son of Usna saw her. Her countenance was purer and clearer than morning-dew upon the rose or the lily, and the rose and lily, nay, the whiteness of the snow of one night and the redness of the reddest rose, were there. Her eyes were blue-black under eyebrows black and fine, but her clustering hair was bright gold, more shining than the gold which boils over the edge of the refiner's crucible. Her forehead was free from all harshness, broad and intelligent, her beautiful smiling lips of the colour of the berries of the mountain ash, her teeth a shower of lustrous pearls. Her face and form, her limbs, hands and feet, were such that no defect, blemish or disproportion could be observed, though one might watch and observe long, seeking to discover them. In that daughter of the High Poet and Historian of the Hound-race of the North, [Footnote: The hound was the type of valour. Though Cuculain was pre-eminently the Hound, the Gaelic equivalents of this word will be discovered in most of the famous names of the cycle.] child of valour and true wisdom, the body did not predominate over the spirit, or the spirit over the body, for as her form was of matchless, incomparable, and inexpressible beauty, so her mind was not a whit less well proportioned and refined. Jocund and happy, breathing innocence and love, she came up the dell. The birds of Angus [Footnote: Angus Ogue's kisses became invisible birds whose singing inspired love.] unseen flew above her and shed upon her unearthly graces and charms from the waving of their immortal wings. A silver brooch lay on her breast, the pin of fine bronze ran straight from one shoulder to the other. On her head was a lustrous tyre or leafy diadem shading her countenance, gold above and silver below. Her short kirtle was white below the rose-red mantle, and fringed with gold thread above her perfect and lightly stepping feet. Shoes she wore shining with brightest wire of findruiney. As she came up the dell, rejoicing in her freedom and the sweetness of that sylvan place and the solitude, she contemplated the bright stream, and sang clear and sweet an unpremeditated song.

Naysi stepped forth from his place, putting aside the ivy with his hands, and came down the dell to meet her in her coming. She did not scream or tremble or show any signs of confusion, though she had never before seen any of the youths of the Gael. She only stood still and straight, and with wide eyes of wonder watched him as he drew nigh, for she thought at first that it was the genius of that glen and torrent taking form in reply to her druidic lay. Then when she recognised the comrade and playfellow of her vision, she smiled a friendly and affectionate greeting. On the other hand, Naysi came trembling and blushing. He bowed himself to the earth before her, and kissed the grass before her feet.

They remained together a long time in the glen and told each other all they knew and thought and felt, save one feeling untellable, happy beyond all power of language to express. When Deirdre rose to go, Naysi asked for some token and symbol of remembrance.

As they went she gathered a rose and gave it to Naysi.

"There is a great meaning in this token amongst the youths and maidens of the Gael," said he.

"I know that," answered Deirdre. Deirdre returned to Levarcam.

"Thou hast gathered the flower," said Levarcam.

"I have," she replied, "and death and life are one to me now, dear foster-mother."

Naysi went away through the forest and there is nothing related concerning him till he reached Dun Usna. It was night when he entered the hall. His brothers were sitting at the central fire. Anli was scouring a shield; Ardane was singing the while he polished a spear and held it out against the light to see its straightness and its lustre. They were in no way alarmed about their brother.

"I have seen Deirdre, the daughter of Felim," he said.

"Then thou art lost!" they answered; the weapons fell from their hands upon the floor.

"I am," he replied.

"What is thy purpose?" they said.

"To storm the guarded dun, even if I go against it alone, To bear away Deirdre and pass into the land of the Albanagh." [Footnote: The Albanagh were the people who inhabited the north and west of Scotland, in fact the Highlanders. In ancient times they and the Irish were regarded as one people.]

"Thou shalt not go alone," they said. "We have shared in thy glory and thy power, we will share all things with thee."

They put their right hand into his on that promise. One hundred and fifty nobles of the nobles of that territory did the same, for with Naysi as their captain they did not fear to go upon any enterprise. They knew that expatriation awaited them, but they had rather be with Naysi and his brothers in a strange land than to live without them in Ireland. So the Clan Usna with their mighty men stormed the dun and bore off Deirdre and went away eastward to the Muirnicht. And they crossed the Moyle [Footnote: The sea between Ireland and Scotland. "Silent, O Moyle. be the roar of thy waters,"] in ships into the country of the Albanagh, and settled on the delightful shores of Loch Etive and made swordland of the surrounding territory. Great, famous, and long remembered were the deeds of the children of Usna in that land.

CHAPTER XI

THERE WAS WAR IN ULSTER

"Each spake words of high disdain
And insult to his heart's best brother,
They parted ne'er to meet again."

COLERIDGE

It was on account of this that there arose at first that
dissidence and divergence of opinion in the great
Council at Emain Macha between Concobar Mac
Nessa and Fergus Mac Roy, Concobar standing for the
law which he had been sworn to safeguard and to
execute, and Fergus casting over the lovers the shield
of his name and fame, his authority and his strength,
and the singular affection with which he was regarded
by all the Ultonians.

After Fergus had made that speech in disparagement
and contempt of the solemn enactment and decree in
accordance with which Deirdre had been immured,
Concobar did not immediately answer, for he knew
that he was heated both on account of the abduction
and on account of the words of Fergus. Then he said -

"The valour of the Red Branch, whereby we flourish so

Standish O'Grady

conspicuously herein the North, doth not spring out of itself, and doth not come by discipline, teaching, and example. It has its root in a virtue of which the bards indeed, for bardic reasons, make little mention though it hold a firm place in the laws of the Ultonians both ancient and recent. This, our valour, and the famous kindred virtues through which we are strong and irresistible, so that the world has today nothing anywhere of equal glory and power, spring from the chastity of our women, which is conspicuous and clear-shining, and in the modesty and shamefastness of our young heroes, and the extreme rarity of lawless relations between men and women in Ulla, the servile tribes excepted, of whom no man maketh any account. Against such lawlessness our wise ancestors have decreed terrible punishments. According to the laws of the Ultonians, those who offend in this respect are burned alive in the place of the burnings, and over their ashes are thrown the three throws of dishonour. And well I know that these laws ofttimes to the unthinking and to those who judge by their affections merely, seem harsh and unnatural. Yea truly, were I not high King, I could weep, seeing gentle youths and maidens, and men and women, whom the singing of Angus Ogue's birds have made mad, led away by my orders to be devoured by flame. But so it is best, for without chastity valour faileth in a nation, and lawlessness in this respect begetteth sure and rapid decay, and I give not this forth as an opinion but as a thing that I know, seeing it as clearly with my mind, O Fergus, as I see with my eyes thy countenance and form and the foldings of thy fuan [Footnote: Mantle.] and the shape and ornamentation of the wheel-brooch upon thy breast. Without chastity there is no enduring valour in a nation. And thou, too, O Fergus, sitting there in the champion's throne, hast more than once or twice heard me pronounce the dread sentence without word of protest or dissent. But now, because it toucheth thee thyself, strongly and fiercely thy voice of protest is lifted up, and unless I and this Council can over-persuade thee, this thy rebellious purpose will be thy own undoing or that of the Red Branch. Are the sons of Usna dear only to thee? I say they are dearer to me, but the Red Branch is still dearer, and it is the destruction of the Red Branch which unwittingly thou wouldst Compass. Nor was that law concerning the inviolable virginity of the child of Felim foolish or unwise, for it was made solemnly by the Ultonians in obedience to the united voice of the Druids of Ulla, men who see deeply into the hidden causes of things and the obscure relations of events, of which we men of war have no perception."

So spoke Concobar, not threateningly like a sovereign king, but pleadingly. On the other hand Fergus Mac Roy, rearing his huge form, stood upon his feet, and said -

"To answer fine reasonings I have no skill, but I swear by the sun and the wind and the earth and by my own right hand, which is a stronger oath than any, that I will bring back the sons of Usna into Ireland, and that they shall live and flourish in their place and sit honourably in this great hall of the Clanna Rury, whether it be pleasing to thee or displeasing. For I take the Clan Usna under my protection from this day forth, and well I know that there is not in Erin or in Alba a man born of a woman, no nor the Tuatha De Danan themselves, who will break through that protection!"

"I will break through it," said the King.

After that Fergus departed from Emain Macha and went away with his people into the east to his own country. There he debated and considered for a long time, but at last, so great was his affection for the Clan Usna, that he went over the Moyle in ships to the country of the Albanagh and brought home the sons of Usna, and they were slain by Concobar Mac Nessa, according as he had promised by the word of his mouth. Then Fergus rebelled against Concobar, drawing after him two-thirds of the Red Branch, and amongst them Duvac Dael Ulla and Cormac Conlingas, Concobar's own son, and many other great men, but the chiefest and best and most renowned of the Ultonians adhered to the King. The whole province was shaken with war and there was great shedding of blood, but in the end Concobar prevailed and drove out Fergus Mac Roy. After that expulsion Fergus and three thousand of the Red Branch fled across the Shannon and came to Rath Cruhane, and entered into military service with Meave who was the queen of all the country west of the Shannon.

There is nothing told about Cuculain in connection with this war. It is hard to imagine him taking any side in such a war. But, in fact, he was still a schoolboy under tutors and governors and could not lawfully appear in arms, seeing that he was not yet knighted. He was either with the smiths or, having procured a worthy hound to take his place, he had gone back to the royal school at Emain Macha. But the time when Cuculain should be knighted, that is to say, invested with arms, and solemnly received into the Red Branch as man to the high King of all Ulla, now drew on, and such a knighting as that, and under such signs, omens, and portents, has never been recorded anywhere in the history of the nations.

In the meantime, Fergus and his exiles served Queen Meave and were subduing all the rest of Ireland under her authority, so that Meave, Queen of Connaught, became very great and proud, and in the end meditated the overthrow of Ulster and the conquest of the Red Branch. Queen Meave and Fergus leading the joined host of the four remaining provinces, Meath, Connaught, Munster, and Leinster, certain of success owing to a strange lethargy which then fell on the Ultonians, did invade Ulster. But as they drew nigh to the mearings they found the in-gate of the province barred by one man. It is needless to mention that man's name. It was Dethcaen's nursling, the ex-pupil of Fergus Mac Roy, the little boy Setanta grown into a terrible and irresistible hero. It was by his defence of Ulster on that occasion against Fergus and Meave and the four provinces, that Cuculain acquired his deathless glory and became the chief hero of the north-west of the world. So these chapters which relate to the abduction of Deirdre and the rebellion and expulsion of Fergus, are a vital portion of the whole story of Cuculain. We must now return to the hero's schoolboy days which, however, are drawing to a memorable conclusion.

CHAPTER XII

THE SACRED CHARIOT

"He dwelt a while among the neat-herds
Of King Admetus, veiling his godhood."

Greek Mythology.

"At Tailteen I raced my steeds against a woman,
Though great with child she came first to the goal,
Alas, I knew not the auburn-haired Macha,
Thence came affliction upon the Ultonians."

CONCOBAR MAC NESSA.

Concobar Mac Nessa on a solemn day called Cuculain
forth from the ranks of the boys where they stood in
the rear of the assembly and said -

"O Setanta, there is a duty which falls to me by virtue
of my kingly office, and therein I need an assistant. For
it is my province to keep bright and in good running
order the chariot of Macha wherein she used to go
forth to war from Emain, and to clean out the corn-
troughs of her two steeds and put there fresh barley
perpetually, and fresh hay in their mangers. Illan the

Fair [Footnote: He was one of the sons of Fergus Mac Roy slain in the great civil war.] was my last helper in this office, till the recent great rebellion. That ministry is thine now, if it is pleasing to thee to accept it."

The boy said that it was pleasing, and the King gave him the key of the chamber in which were the vessels and implements used in discharging that sacred function.

Afterwards, on the same day, the King said to him, "Wash thyself now in pure water and put on new clean raiment and come again to me."

The boy washed himself and put on new clean raiment. The King himself did the same.

Concobar said: "Go now to the chamber of which I have given thee the key and fill with oil the silver oil-can and take a towel of the towels of fawn-skin which are there and return." He did so; and Concobar and his nephew, armed youths following, went to the house of the chariot.

Ere Concobar turned the wards of the lock he heard voices within in the chariot-house. There, one said to another, "This is he. Our long watch and ward are near the end." And the other said, "It is well. Too long have we been here waiting."

"Hast thou heard anything, my nephew?" said Concobar.

"I have heard nothing," said the lad.

Concobar opened the great folding-doors. There was a

sound there like glad voices mingled with a roar of revolving wheels, and then silence. Setanta drew back in dismay, and even Concobar stood still. "I have not observed such portents before in the chariot-house," he said. The King and his nephew entered the hollow chamber. The chariot was motionless but very bright. One would have said that the bronze burned. It was of great size and beauty. By its side were two horse-stalls with racks and mangers, the bars of the rack were of gold bronze which was called findruiney, and the mangers of yellow brass. The floor was paved with cut marble, the walls lined with smooth boards of ash. There were no windows, but there were nine lamps in the room. "It will be thy duty to feed those lamps," said Concobar.

Concobar took the fawn-skin towel from the boy and polished the chariot, and the wheels, tyres, and boxes, and the wheel-spokes. He oiled the wheels too, and mightily lifting the great chariot seized the spokes with his right hand and made the wheels spin.

"Go now to the chamber of which I have given thee the keys," he said, "and bring the buckets, and clear out the mangers to the last grain, and empty the stale barley into the place of the burning, and afterwards take fresh barley from the bin which is in the chamber and fill the mangers. Empty the racks also and bring fresh hay. Thou wilt find it stored there too; clean straw also and litter the horse-stalls."

The boy did that. In the meantime Concobar polished the pole, and the yoke, and the chains. From the wall he took the head-gear of the horses and the long shining reins of interwoven brass and did the same very carefully till there was not a speck of rust or discolouration to be seen.

"Where are the horses, my Uncle Concobar?" said the boy.

"That I cannot rightly tell," said Concobar, "but verily they are somewhere."

"What are those horses?" said the boy. "How are they called? What their attributes, and why do I fill their racks and mangers?"

"They are the Liath Macha and Black Shanglan," said Concobar. "They have not been seen in Erin for three hundred years, not since Macha dwelt visibly in Emain as the bride of Kimbaoth, son of Fiontann. In this chariot she went forth to war, charioteering her warlike groom. But they are to come again for the promised one and bear him to battle and to conflict in this chariot, and the time is not known but the King of Emain is under gesa [Footnote: Terrible druidic obligations.] to keep the chariot bright and the racks and mangers furnished with fresh hay, and barley two years old. He is to wait, and watch, and stand prepared under gesa most terrible."

"Maybe Kimbaoth will return to us again," said the boy.

"Nay, it hath not been so prophesied," answered the King. "He was great, and stern, and formidable. But our promised one is gentle exceedingly. He will not know his own greatness, and his nearest comrades will not know it, and there will be more of love in his heart than war." So saying Concobar looked steadfastly upon the boy.

"Conall Carnach is as famous for love as for war," said Setanta. "He is peerless in beauty, and his strength and courage are equal to his comeliness, and his chivalry and battle-splendour to his strength."

"Nay, lad, it is not Conall Carnach, though the women of Ulla sicken and droop for the love of him. Verily, it is not Conall Carnach."

Setanta examined curiously the great war-car.

"Was Kimbaoth assisting his wife," he asked, "when she took captive the sons of Dithorba?"

"Nay," said the King, "she went forth alone and crossed the Shannon with one step into the land of the Fir-bolgs, and there, one by one, she bound those builder-giants the sons of Dithorba, and bore them hither in her might, and truly those five brethren were no small load for the back of one woman."

"Has anyone seen her in our time?" asked the lad.

"I have," said Concobar. "I saw her at the great fair of Tailteen. There she pronounced a curse upon me and upon the Red Branch. [Footnote: At Tailteen a man boasted that his wife could outrun Concobar's victorious chariot-steeds. Concobar compelled the woman to run against his horses. She won the race, but died at the goal leaving her curse upon the Red Branch.] The curse hath not yet fallen, but it will fall in my time, and the promised one will come in my time and he will redeem us from its power. Great tribulation will be his. Question me no more, dear Setanta, I have said more than enough."

They went forth from the sacred chamber and Concobar locked the doors.

As they crossed the vacant space going to the palace, Concobar said -

"Why art thou sad, dear Setanta?"

"I am not sad," answered the boy.

"Truly there is no sadness in thy face, or thy lips, in thy voice or thy behaviour, but it is deep down in thine eyes," said the King. "I see it there always."

Setanta laughed lightly. "I know it not," he said.

Concobar went his way after that, musing, and Setanta, having replaced the sacred vessels in their chamber and having locked the door, strode away into the boys' hall. There was a great fire in the midst, and the boys sat round it, for it was cold. Cuculain broke their circle, pushing the boys asunder, and sat down. They tried to drag him away, but he laughed and kept his place like a rock. Then they called him "a Fomorian, and no man," and perforce made their circle wider.

CHAPTER XIII

THE WEIRD HORSES

"On the brink of the night and the morning
My coursers are wont to respire,
But the earth has just whispered a warning,
That their flight must be swifter than fire,
They shall breathe the hot air of desire."

SHELLEY.

One night when the stars shone brightly, Setanta, as he passed by Cathvah's astrological tower, heard him declare to his students that whoever should be knighted by Concobar on a certain day would be famous to the world's end. He was in his coming out of the forest then with a bundle of young ash trees under his arm. He thought to put them to season and therewith make slings, for truly he surpassed all others in the use of the sling. Setanta went his way after that and came into the speckled house. It was the armoury of the Red Branch and shone with all manner of war-furniture. A fire burned here always, absorbing the damp of the air lest the metal should take rust. Setanta flung his trees into the rafters over the fire very deftly, so that they caught and remained there. He said they would season best in that place.

As he turned to go a man stood before him in the vast and hollow chamber.

"I know thee," said the boy. "What wouldst thou now?"

"Thou shalt go forth to-night," said the man, [Footnote: This man was Lu the Long-Handed, the same who met him when he was leaving home.] "and take captive the Liath Macha and Black Shanghlan. Power will be given to thee. Go out boldly."

"I am not wont to go out fearfully," answered the lad. "Great labours are thrust upon me."

He went into the supper hall as at other times and took his customary place there, and ate and drank.

"Thy eyes are very bright," said Laeg.

"They will be brighter ere the day," he replied.

"That is an expert juggler," said Laeg. "How he tosseth the bright balls!"

"Can he toss the stars so?" said Setanta.

"Thou art strange and wild to-night," said Laeg.

"I will be stranger and wilder ere the morrow," cried Setanta.

He stood up to go. Laeg caught him by the skirt of his mantle. The piece came away in his hand.

"Whither art thou going, Setanta?" cried the King from

the other end of the vast hall.

"To seek my horses," cried the lad. His voice rang round the hollow dome and down the resounding galleries and long corridors, so that men started in their seats and looked towards him.

"They are stabled since the setting of the sun," said the chief groom.

"Thou liest," answered the boy. "They are in the hills and valleys of Erin." His eyes burned like fire and his stature was exalted before their eyes.

"Great deeds will be done in Erin this night," said Concobar.

He went forth into the night. There was great power upon him. He crossed the Plain of the Hurlings and the Plain of the Assemblies and the open country and the great waste moor, going on to Dun-Culain. Culain's new hound cowered low when he saw him. The boy sprang over moat and rampart at one bound and burst open the doors of the smith's house, breaking the bar. The noise of the riven beam was like the brattling of thunder.

"That is an unusual way to enter a man's house," said Culain. He and his people were at supper.

"It is," said Setanta. "Things more unusual will happen this night. Give me bridles that will hold the strongest horses." Culain gave him two bridles.

"Will they hold the strongest horses?" said the boy.

"Anything less than the Liath Macha they will hold," said the smith.

The boy snapped the bridles and flung them aside. "I want bridles that will hold the Liath Macha and Black Shanglan," said he.

"Fire all the furnaces," cried Culain. "Handle your tools; show your might. Work now, men, for your lives. Verily, if he get not the bridles, soon your dead will be more numerous than your living."

Culain and his people made the bridles. He gave them to Cuculain. The smiths stood around in pallid groups. Cuculain took the bridles and went forth. He went south-westwards to Slieve Fuad, and came to the Grey Lake. The moon shone and the lake glowed like silver. There was a great horse feeding by the lake. He raised his head and neighed when he heard footsteps on the hill. He came on against Cuculain and Cuculain went on against him. The boy had one bridle knotted round his waist and the other in his teeth. He leaped upon the steed and caught him by the forelock and his mouth. The horse reared mightily, but Setanta held him and dragged his head down to the ground. The grey steed grew greater and more terrible. So did Cuculain.

"Thou hast met thy master, O Liath Macha, this night," he cried. "Surely I will not lose thee. Ascend into the heavens, or, breaking the earth's roof, descend to Orchil, [Footnote: A great sorceress who ruled the world under the earth.] yet even so thou wilt not shake me away."

Ireland quaked from the centre to the sea. They reeled together, steed and hero, through the plains of

Murthemney. "Make the circuit of Ireland Liath Macha and I shall be on the neck of thee," cried Cuculain. The horse went in reeling circles round Ireland. Cuculain mightily thust the bit into his mouth and made fast the headstall. The Liath Macha went a second time round Ireland. The sea retreated from the shore and stood in heaps. Cuculain sprang upon his back. A third time the horse went round Ireland, bounding from peak to peak. They seemed a resplendent Fomorian phantom against the stars. The horse came to a stand. "I think thou art tamed, O Liath Macha," said Cuculain. "Go on now to the Dark Valley." They came to the Dark Valley. There was night there always. Shapes of Death and Horror, Fomorian apparitions, guarded the entrance. They came against Cuculain, and he went against them. A voice from within cried, "Forbear, this is the promised one. Your watching and warding are at end." He rode into the Dark Valley. There was a roaring of unseen rivers in the darkness, of black cataracts rushing down the steep sides of the Valley. The Liath Macha neighed loudly. The neigh reverberated through the long Valley. A horse neighed joyfully in response. There was a noise of iron doors rushing open some- where, and a four-footed thunderous trampling on the hollow-sounding earth. A steed came to the Liath Macha. Cuculain felt for his head in the dark, and bitted and bridled him ere he was aware. The horse reared and struggled. The Liath Macha dragged him down the Valley. "Struggle not, Black Shanglan," said Cuculain, "I have tamed thy better." The horse ceased to struggle. Down and out of the Dark Valley rodest thou, O peerless one, with thy horses. The Liath Macha was grey to whiteness, the other horse was black and glistening like the bright mail of the chaffer. He rode thence to Emain Macha with the two horses like a lord of Day and Night, and of Life and Death. Truly the might and power of the Long-Handed and Far-Shooting one was upon him that night. He came to Emain Macha. The doors of Macha's stable flew open before him. He rode the horses into the stable. Macha's war-car brayed forth a brazen roar of welcome, the Tuatha De Danan shouted, and the car itself glowed and sparkled. The horses went to their ancient stalls, the Liath Macha to that which was nearer to the door. Cuculain took off their bridles and hanged them on the wall. He went forth into the night. The horses were already eating their barley, but they looked after him as he went. The doors shut to with a brazen clash. Cuculain stood alone in the great court under the stars. A druidic storm was abroad and howled in the forests. He thought all that had taken place a wild dream. He went to his dormitory and to his couch. Laeg was asleep with the starlight shining on his white forehead; his red hair was shed over the pillow. Cuculain kissed him, and sitting on the bed's edge wept. Laeg awoke.

"Thou wert not well at supper," said Laeg, "and now thou hast been wandering in the damp of the night, and thou with a fever upon thee, for I hear thy teeth clattering. I sought to hinder thee, and thou wouldst not be persuaded. Verily, if thou wilt not again obey me, being thy senior, thou shalt have sore bones at my hands. Undress thyself now and come to bed without delay."

Cuculain did so.

"Thou art as cold as ice," said Laeg.

"Nay, I am hotter than fire," said Cuculain.

"Thou art ice, I say," said Laeg, "and thy teeth are

Standish O'Grady

clattering like hailstones on a brazen shield. Ay, and thine eyes shine terribly."

Laeg started from the couch. He struck flintsparks upon a rag steeped in nitre, and waved it to a flame, and kindled a lanthorn. He flung his own mantle upon the bed and went forth in his shirt. The storm raged terribly; the stars were dancing in high heaven. He came to the house of the Chief Leech and beat at the door. The Leech was not in bed. All the wise men of Emain Macha were awake that night, listening to the portents.

"Setanta, son of Sualtam, is sick," said Laeg.

"What are his symptoms?" said the Leech.

"He is colder than ice, his eyes shine terribly, and his teeth clatter, but he says that he is hotter than fire."

The Leech went to Cuculain. "This is not a work for me," he said, "but for a seer. Bring hither Cathvah and his Druids." Cathvah and and his seers came. They made their symbols of power over the youth and chanted their incantations and Druid songs. After that Cuculain slept. He slept for three days and three nights. There was a great stillness while the boy slept, for it was not lawful at any time for anyone to awake Cuculain when he slumbered.

On the third morning Cuculain awoke. The bright morning sunshine was all around, and the birds sang in Emain Macha. He called for Laeg with a loud voice and bade him order a division of the boys to get ready their horses and chariots for charioteering exercise and fighting out of their cars.

CHAPTER XIV

THE KNIGHTING OF CUCULAIN

"Then felt I like a watcher of the skies
When a new planet swims into his ken."

KEATS.

The prophecies concerning the coming of some extraordinary warrior amongst the Red Branch had been many and ancient, and by certain signs Concobar believed that his time was now near. Often he contemplated his nephew, observed his beauty, his strength, and his unusual proficiency in all martial exercises, and mused deeply considering the omens. But when he saw him slinging and charioteering amongst the rest, shooting spears and casting battle-stones at a mark before the palace upon the lawn, and saw him eating and drinking before him nightly in the hall like another, and heard his clear voice and laughter amongst the boys, his schoolfellows and comrades, then the thought or the faint surmise or wish that his nephew might be that promised one passed out of his mind, for the prophesyings and the rumours had been very great, and men looked for one who should resemble Lu the Long-Handed, son of Ethlend, [Footnote: This great deity resembled the Greek

Phoebus Apollo. He led the rebellion of the gods against the Fomorian giants who had previously reduced them to a condition of intolerable slavery. Some say that he was Cuculain's true father. His favourite weapon was the sling, likened here to the rainbow. It was not a thong or cord sling, but a pliant rod such as boys in Ireland still make. The milky way was his chain.] whose sling was like the cloud bow, who thundered and lightened against the giants of the Fomoroh, who was all power and all skill, whose chain wherewith he used to confine Tuatha De Danan and Milesians, spanned the midnight sky. The rumours and prophecies were indeed exceeding great and Cuculain, though he far surpassed the rest, was but a boy like others. He stood at the head of Concobar's horses when the King ascended his chariot. His shoulder was warm and firm to the touch when the King lightly laid his hand upon him.

One night there were terrible portents. All Ireland quaked; there was a druidic storm under bright stars; the buildings rocked; a brazen clangour sounded from the Tec Brac; there were mighty tramplings and cries and a four-footed thunder of giant hoofs, and they went round Ireland three times, only the third time swifter and like a hurricane of sound. Cuculain was abroad that night. There was deep sleep upon the people of Emain, only the chiefs were awake and aware. Cuculain was sick after that. The Druids stood around his bed.

"The world labours with the new birth," said Concobar. "Maybe my nephew is the forerunner, the herald and announcer of the coming god!"

One evening, after supper, when the lad came to bid

his uncle good-night as his custom was, he said, "If it be pleasing to thee, my Uncle Concobar, I would be knighted on the morrow, for I am now of due age, and owing to the instructions of my tutor, Fergus Mac Roy, and thyself, and my other teachers and instructors, I am thought to be sufficiently versed in martial exercises, and able to play a man's part amongst the Red Branch."

He was now a man's full height, but his face was a boy's face, and his strength and agility amazed all who observed him in his exercises.

"Has thou heard what Cathvah has predicted concerning the youth who is knighted on that day?" said the King.

"Yes," answered the lad.

"That he will be famous and short-lived and unhappy?"

"Truly," he replied.

"And doth thy purpose still hold?"

"Yes," he answered, "but whether it be mine I cannot tell."

Concobar, though unwilling, yielded to that request.

Loegairey, the Victorious, son of Conud, son of Iliach, the second best knight of the Red Branch and the most devoted to poetry of them all came that night into the hall while the rest slumbered. The candles were flickering in their sockets. Darkness invested the rest of the vast hollow-sounding chamber, but there was light around the throne and couch of the King, owing to the splendour of the pillars and of the canopy shining with bronze, white and red, and silver and gold, and glittering with carbuncles and diamonds, and owing to the light which always surrounded the King and encircled his regal head like a luminous cloud, seen by many. He was looking straight out before him with bright eyes, considering and consulting for the Red Branch while they slept. Two great men having their swords drawn in their hands, stood behind him, on the right and on the left, like statues, motionless and silent.

Loegairey drew nigh to the King. Distraction and amazement were in his face. His dense and lustrous hair was dishevelled and in agitation round his neck and huge shoulders. He held in his hand two long spears with rings of walrus tooth where the timber met the shank of the flashing blades; they trembled in his hand. His lips were dry, his voice very low.

"There are horses in the stable of Macha," he said.

"I know it," answered the King.

Concobar called for water, and when he had washed his hands and his face, he took from its place the chess-board of the realm, arranged the men, and observed their movements and combinations. He closed the board and put the men in their net of bronze wire, and restored all to their place.

"Great things will happen on the morrow, O grandson of Iliach," he said. "Take candles and go before me to the boys' dormitory."

They went to the boys' dormitory and to the couch of

Cuculain. Cuculain and Laeg were asleep together there. Their faces towards each other and their hair mingled together. Cuculain's face was very tranquil, and his breathing inaudible, like an infant's.

"O sweet and serene face," murmured the King, "I see great clouds of sorrow coming upon you."

They returned to the hall.

"Go now to thy rest and thy slumber, O Loegairey," said the King. "When the curse of Macha descends upon us I know one who will withstand it."

"Surely it is not that stripling?" said Loegairey. But the King made no answer.

On the morrow there was a great hosting of the Red Branch on the plain of the Assemblies. It was May-Day morning and the sun shone brightly, but at first through radiant showers. The trees were putting forth young buds; the wet grass sparkled. All the martial pomp and glory of the Ultonians were exhibited that day. Their chariots and war-horses ringed the plain. All the horses' heads were turned towards the centre where were Concobar Mac Nessa and the chiefs of the Red Branch. The plain flashed with gold, bronze, and steel, and glowed with the bright mantles of the innumerable heroes, crimson and scarlet, blue, green, or purple. The huge brooches on their breasts of gold and silver or gold-like bronze, were like resplendent wheels. Their long hair, yellow for the most part, was bound with ornaments of gold. Great, truly, were those men, their like has not come since upon the earth. They were the heroes and demigods of the heroic age of Erin, champions who feared nought beneath the sun, mightiest among the mighty, huge, proud, and unconquerable, and loyal and affectionate beyond all others; all of the blood of Ir, [Footnote: On account of their descent from Ir, son of Milesius, the Red Branch were also called the Irians.] son of Milesius, the Clanna Rury of great renown, rejoicing in their valour, their splendour, their fame and their peerless king. Concobar had no crown. A plain circle of beaten gold girt his broad temples. In the naked glory of his regal manhood he stood there before them all, but even so a stranger would have swiftly discovered the captain of the Red Branch, such was his stature, his bearing, such his slowly-turning, steady-gazing eyes and the majesty of his bearded countenance. His countenance was long, broad above and narrow below, his nose eminent, his beard bipartite, curling and auburn in hue, his form without any blemish or imperfection.

Cuculain came forth from the palace. He wore that day a short mantle of pale-red silk bordered with white thread and fastened on the breast with a small brooch like a wheel of silver. The hues upon that silk were never the same. His tunic of fine linen was girt at the waist with a leathern zone, stained to the resemblance of the wild-briar rose. It descended to but did not pass his beautiful knees, falling into many plaits. The tunic was cut low at the neck, exposing his throat and the knot in the throat and the cup-shaped indentation above the breast. On his feet were comely shoes sparkling with bronze plates. They took the colour of everything which they approached. His hair fell in many curls over the pale-red mantle, without adornment or confinement. It was the colour of the flower which is named after the dearest Disciple, but which was called sovarchey by the Gael. A tinge of red ran through the gold. As to his eyes, no two men or women could agree concerning their colour, for some said they were blue, and some grey, and others hazel; and there were those who said that they were blacker than the blackest night that was ever known. Yet again, there were those who said that they were of all colours named and nameless. They were soft and liquid splendours, unfathomable lakes of light above his full and ruddy cheeks, and beneath his curved and most tranquil brows. In form he was symmetrical, straight and pliant as a young fir tree when the sweet spring sap fills its veins. So he came to that assembly, in the glory of youth, beauty, strength, valour, and beautiful shame-fastness, yet proud in his humility and glittering like the morning star. Choice youths, his comrades, attended him. The kings held their breaths when he drew nigh, moving white knee after white knee over the green and sparkling grass. When the other rites had been performed and the due sacrifices and libations made, and after Cuculain had put his right hand into the right hand of the King and become his man, Concobar gave him a shield, two spears and a sword, weapons of great price and of thrice proved excellence - a strong man's equipment. Cuculain struck the spears together at right angles and broke them. He clashed the sword flat-wise on the shield. The sword leaped into small pieces and the shield was bent inwards and torn.

"These are not good weapons, my King," said the boy. Then the King gave him others, larger and stronger and worthy of his best champions. These, too, the boy broke into pieces in like manner.

"Son of Nessa, these are still worse," he said, "nor is it well done, O Captain of the Red Branch, to make me a laughing-stock in the presence of this great hosting of the Ultonians."

Concobar Mac Nessa exulted exceedingly when he beheld the amazing strength and the waywardness of the boy, and beneath delicate brows his eyes glittered like glittering swords as he glanced proudly round on the crowd of martial men that surrounded him. Amongst them all he seemed himself a bright torch of valour and war, more pure and clear than polished steel. He then beckoned to one of his knights, who hastened away and returned bringing Concobar's own shield and spears and sword out of the Tec Brac, where they were kept, an equipment in reserve. And Cuculain shook them and bent them and clashed them together, but they held firm.

"These are good arms, O son of Nessa," said Cuculain.

"Choose now thy charioteer," said the King, "for I will give thee also war-horses and a chariot."

He caused to pass before Cuculain all the boys who in many and severe tests had proved their proficiency in charioteering, in the management and tending of steeds, in the care of weapons and steed-harness, and all that related to charioteering science. Amongst them was Laeg, with a pale face and dejected, his eyes red and his cheeks stained from much weeping. Cuculain laughed when he saw him, and called him forth from the rest, naming him by his name with a loud, clear voice, heard to the utmost limit of the great host.

"There was fear upon thee," said Cuculain.

"There is fear upon thyself," answered Laeg. "It was in thy mind that I would refuse."

"Nay, there is no such fear upon me," said Cuculain.

"Then there is fear upon me," said Laeg. "A charioteer needs a champion who is stout and a valiant and faithful. Yea, truly there is fear upon me," answered Laeg.

"Verily, dear comrade and bed-fellow," answered Cuculain, "it is through me that thou shalt get thy death-wound, and I say not this as a vaunt, but as a prophecy."

And that prophecy was fulfilled, for the spear that slew Laeg went through his master.

After that Laeg stood by Cuculain's side and held his peace, but his face shone with excess of joy and pride. He wore a light graceful frock of deerskin, joined in the front with a twine of bronze wire, and a short, dark-red cape, secured by a pin of gold with a ring to it. A band of gold thread confined his auburn hair, rising into a peak behind his head. In his hands he held a goad of polished red-yew, furnished with a crooked hand-grip of gold, and pointed with shining bronze, and where the bronze met the timber there was a circlet of diamond of the diamonds of Banba. He had also a short-handled scourge with a haft of walrus tooth, and the rope, cord, and lash of that scourge were made of delicate and delicately-twisted thread of copper. This equipment was the equipment of a proved charioteer; the apprentices wore only grey capes with white fringes, fastened by loops of red cord.

Laeg was one of three brothers, all famous charioteers. Id and Sheeling were the others. They were all three sons of the King of Gabra, whose bright dun arose upon a green and sloping hill over against Tara towards the rising of the sun. Thence sprang the beautiful stream of the Nemnich, rich in lilies and reeds and bulrushes, which to-day men call the Nanny Water. Laeg was grey-eyed and freckled.

Then there were led forward by two strong knights a pair of great and spirited horses and a splendid war-car. The King said, "They are thine, dear nephew. Well I know that neither thou, nor Laeg, will be a dishonour to this war equipage."

Cuculain sprang into the car, and standing with legs apart, he stamped from side to side and shook the car mightily, till the axle brake, and the car itself was broken in pieces.

"It is not a good chariot," said the lad.

Another was led forward, and he broke it in like manner.

"Give me a sound chariot, High Lord of the Clanna Rury, or give me none," he said. "No prudent warrior would fight from such brittle foothold."

He brake in succession nine war chariots, the greatest and strongest in Emain. When he broke the ninth the horses of Macha neighed from their stable. Great fear fell upon the host when they heard that unusual noise and the reverberation of it in the woods and hills.

"Let those horses be harnessed to the Chariot of Macha," cried Concobar, "and let Laeg, son of the King of Gabra, drive them hither, for those are the horses and that the chariot which shall be given this day to Cuculain."

Then, son of Sualtam, how in thy guileless breast thy heart leaped, when thou heardest the thundering of the great war-car and the wild neighing of the immortal steeds, as they broke from the dark stable into the clear-shining light of day, and heard behind them the ancient roaring of the brazen wheels as in the days when they bore forth Macha and her martial groom against the giants of old, and mightily established in Eiriu the Red Branch of the Ultonians! Soon they rushed to view from the rear of Emain, speeding forth impetuously out of the hollow-sounding ways of the city and the echoing palaces into the open, and behind them in the great car green and gold, above the many-twinkling wheels, the charioteer, with floating mantle, girt round the temples with the gold fillet of his office, leaning backwards and sideways as he laboured to restrain their fury unrestrainable; a grey long-maned steed, whale-bellied, broad-chested, with mane like flying foam, under one silver yoke, and a black lustrous, tufty-maned steed under the other, such steeds as in power, size, and beauty the earth never produced before and never will produce again.

Like a hawk swooping along the face of a cliff when the wind is high, or like the rush of March wind over the smooth plain, or like the fleetness of the stag roused from his lair by the hounds and covering his first field, was the rush of those steeds when they had broken through the restraint of the charioteer, as though they galloped over fiery flags, so that the earth shook and trembled with the velocity of their motion, and all the time the great car brayed and shrieked as the wheels of solid and glittering bronze went round, and strange cries and exclamations were heard, for they were demons that had their abode in that car.

The charioteer restrained the steeds before the assembly, but nay-the-less a deep purr, like the purr of a tiger, proceeded from the axle. Then the whole assembly lifted up their voices and shouted for Cuculain, and he himself, Cuculain, the son of Sualtam, sprang into his chariot, all armed, with a cry as of a warrior springing into his chariot in the battle, and he stood erect and brandished his spears, and the war sprites of the Gael shouted along with him, for the Bocanahs and Bananahs and the Geniti Glindi, the wild people of the glens, and the demons of the air, roared around him, when first the great warrior of the Gael, his battle-arms in his hands, stood equipped for war in his chariot before all the warriors of his tribe, the kings of the Clanna Rury and the people of Emain Macha. Then, too, there sounded from the Tec Brac the boom of shields, and the clashing of swords and the cries and shouting of the Tuatha De Danan, who dwelt there perpetually; and Lu the Long-Handed, the slayer of Balor, the destroyer of the Fomoroh, the immortal, the invisible, the maker and decorator of the Firmament, whose hound was the sun and whose son the viewless wind, thundered from heaven and bent his sling five-hued against the clouds; and the son of the illimitable Lir [Footnote: Mananan mac Lir, the sea-god.] in his mantle blue and green, foam-fringed passed through the assembly with a roar of far-off innumerable waters, and the Mor Reega stood in the midst with a foot on either side of the plain, and shouted with the shout of a host, so that the Ultonians fell down like reaped grass with their faces to the earth, on account of the presence of the Mor Reega, and on account of the omens and great signs.

Cuculain bade Laeg let the steeds go. They went like a storm and three times encircled Emain Macha. It was the custom of the Ultonians to march thrice round Emain ere they went forth to war.

Then said Cuculain - "Whither leads the great road yonder?"

"To Ath-na-Forairey and the borders of the Crave Rue."

"And wherefore is it called the Ford of the Watchings?" said Cuculain.

"Because," answered Laeg, "there is always one of the King's knights there, keeping watch and ward over the gate of the province."

"Guide thither the horses," said Cuculain, "for I will not lay aside my arms till I have first reddened them in the blood of the enemies of my nation. Who is it that is over the ward there this day?"

"It is Conall Carnach," said Laeg.

As they drew nigh to the ford, the watchman from his high watch-tower on the west side of the dun sent forth a loud and clear voice -

"There is a chariot coming to us from Emain Macha," he said. "The chariot is of great size; I have not seen its like in all Eiriu. In front of it are two horses, one black and one white. Great is their trampling and their glory and the shaking of their heads and necks. I liken their progress to the fall of water from a high cliff or the sweeping of dust and beech-tree leaves over a plain, when the March wind blows hard, or to the rapidity of thunder rattling over the firmament. A man would say that there were eight legs under each horse, so rapid and indistinguishable is the motion of their limbs and hoofs. Identify those horses, O Conall, and that chariot, for to me they are unknown."

"And to me likewise," said Conall. "Who are in the chariot? Moderate, O man, the extravagance of thy language, for thou art not a prophet but a watchman."

"There are two beardless youths in the chariot," answered the watchman, "but I am unable to identify them on account of the dust and the rapid motion and the steam of the horses. I think the charioteer is Laeg, the son of the King of Gabra, for I know his manner of driving. The boy who sits in front of him and below him on the champion's seat I do not know, but he shines like a star in the cloud of dust and steam." Then a young man who stood near to Conall Carna, wearing a short, red cloak with a blue hood to it, and a tassel at the point of the hood, said to Conall -

"If it be my brother that charioteers sure am I that it is Cuculain who is in the fighter's seat, for many a time have I heard Laeg utter foul scorn of the Red Branch, none excepted, when compared with Sualtam's son. For no other than him would he deign to charioteer. Truly though he is my own brother there is not such a boaster in the North."

Then the watchman cried out again -

"Yea, the charioteer is the son of the King of Gabra, and it is Cuculain, the son of Sualtam, who sits in the fighter's seat. He has Concobar's own shield on his breast, and his two spears in his hand. Over Bray Ros, over Brainia, they are coming along the highway, by the foot of the Town of the Tree; it is gifted with victories."

"Have done, O talkative man," cried Conall, "whose words are like the words of a seer, or the full-voiced intonement of a chief bard."

When the chariot came to the ford, Conall was amazed at the horses and the chariot, but he dissembled his amazement before his people, and when he saw Cuculain armed, he laughed and said, -

"Hath the boy indeed taken arms?"

And Cuculain said, "It is as thou seest, O son of Amargin; and moreover, I have sworn not to let them back into the Chamber-of-Many-Colours [Footnote: Tec Brac or Speckled House, the armoury of the Ultonians.] until I shall have first reddened them in the blood of the enemies of Ulla."

Then Conall ceased laughing and said, "Not so, Setanta, for verily thou shalt not be permitted;" and the great Champion sprang forward to lay his fearless, never-foiled, and all conquering hands on the bridles of the horses, but at a nod from Cuculain, Laeg let the steeds go, and Conall sprang aside out of the way, so terrible was the appearance of the horses as they reared against him. "Harness my horses and yoke my chariot," cried Conall, "for if this mad boy goes into the enemies' country and meets with harm there, verily I shall never be forgiven by the Ultonians."

His horses were harnessed and his chariot yoked, - illustrious too were those horses, named and famed in many songs - and Conall and Ide in their chariot dashed through the ford enveloped with rainbow-painted clouds of foam and spray, and like hawks on the wing they skimmed the plain, pursuing the boys. Laeg heard the roar and trampling, and looking back over his shoulder, said, -

"They are after us, dear master, namely the great son of Amargin and my haughty brother Ide, who hath ever borne himself to me as though I were a wayward child. They would spoil upon us this our brave foray. But they will overtake the wind sooner than they will overtake the Liath Macha and Black Shanglan, whose going truly is like the going of eagles. O storm-footed steeds, great is my love for you, and inexpressible my pride in your might and your beauty, your speed and your terror, and sweet docility and affection."

"Nevertheless, O Laeg," said Cuculain, "slacken now their going, for that Champion will be an impediment to us in our challengings and our fightings; for when we stop for that purpose he will overtake us, and, be our feats what they may, his and not ours will be the glory. Slacken the going of the horses, for we must rid ourselves of the annoyance and the pursuit of these gadflies."

Laeg slackened the pace, and as they went Cuculain leaped lightly from his seat and as lightly bounded back again, holding a great pebble in his hand, such as a man using all his strength could with difficulty raise from the ground, and sat still, rejoicing in his purpose, and grasping the pebble with his five fingers.

Conall and Ide came up to them after that, and Conall, as the senior and the best man amongst the Ultonians, clamorously called to them to turn back straightway, or he would hough their horses, or draw the linch-pins of their wheels, or in some other manner bring their foray to naught. Cuculain thereupon stood upright in the car, and so standing, with feet apart to steady him in his throwing and in his aim, dashed the stone upon the yoke of Conall's chariot between the heads of the horses and broke the yoke, so that the pole fell to the ground and the chariot tilted forward violently. Then the charioteer fell amongst the horses, and Conall Carna, the beauty of the Ultonians the battle-winning and ever-victorious son of Amargin, was shot out in front upon the road, and fell there upon his left shoulder, and his beautiful raiment was defiled with dust; and when he arose his left hand hung by his side, for the shoulder-bone was driven from the socket, owing to the violence of the fall.

"I swear by all my gods," he cried, "that if a step would save thy head from the hands of the men of Meath, I would not take it."

Cuculain laughed and replied, "Good, O Conall, and who asked thee to take it, or craved of thee any succour or countenance? Was it a straight shot? Are there the materials of a fighter in me at all, dost thou think? Thou art in my debt now too, O Conall. I have saved thee a broken vow, for it is one of the oaths of our Order not to enter hostile territory with brittle chariot-gear!"

Then the boys laughed at him again, and Laeg let go the steeds, and very soon they were out of sight. Conall returned slowly with his broken chariot to Ath-na-Forairey and sent for Fingin of Slieve Fuad, who was the most cunning physician and most expert of bone-setters amongst the Ultonians. Conall's messengers experienced no difficulty in finding the house of the leech, which was very recognisable on account of its shape and appearance, and because it had wide open doors, four in number, affording a liberal ingress and free thoroughfare to all the winds. Also a stream of pure water ran through the house, derived from a well of healing properties, which sprang from the side of the uninhabited hill. Such were the signs that showed the house of a leech.

When they drew nigh they heard the voice of one man talking and of another who laughed. It happened that that day there had been borne thither a champion, in whose body there was not one small bone unbroken or uninjured. The man's bruises and fractures had been dressed and set by Fingin and his intelligent and deft-handed apprentices, and he lay now in his bed of healing listening joyfully to the conversation of the leech, who was beyond all others eloquent and of most agreeable discourse.

When Conall's messengers related the reason of their coming, Fingin cried to his young men, "Harness me my horses and yoke my chariot. There are few," he said, "in Erin for whom I would leave my own house, but that youth is one of them. His father Amargin was well known to me. He was a warrior grim and dour exceedingly, and he ever said concerning the boy, 'This hound's whelp that I have gotten is too fine and sleek to hold bloody gaps or hunt down a noble prey. He will be a women's playmate and not a peer amongst Heroes.' And that fear was ever upon him till the day when Conall came red out of the Valley of the Thrush, and his track thence to Rath-Amargin was one straight path of blood, and he with his shield-arm hacked to the bone, his sword-arm swollen and bursting, and the flame of his valour burning bright in his splendid eyes. Then, for the first time, the old man smiled upon him, and he said, 'That arm, my son, has done a man's work to-day.'"

Standish O'Grady

CHAPTER XV

ACROSS THE MEARINGS AND AWAY

"Say, rushed the bold eagle exultingly forth.
From his home, in the dark rolling clouds of the
North?"

CAMPBELL.

As for the boys, they proceeded joyfully after that
pleasant skirmish and friendly encounter, both on
account of the discomfiture of him who was reckoned
the prime champion of the Ultonians, and because they
were at large in Erin, with no one to direct them, or to
whom they should render an account; and their
happiness, too, was increased by the mettle, power and
gallant action of the steeds, and by the clanking of the
harness and the brazen chains, and the ringing of the
weapons of war, and the roar of the revolving wheels,
and owing to the velocity of their motion and the
rushing of the wind upon their temples and through
their hair.

Then Cuculain stood up in the chariot, and surveyed
the land on all sides, and said -

"What is that great, firm-based, indestructible

mountain upon our left hand, one of a noble range which, rising from the green plain, runs eastward. The last peak there is the mountain of which I speak, whose foot is in the Ictian sea and whose head neighbours the firmament."

And Laeg said, "Men call it Slieve Modurn, after a giant of the elder time, when men were mightier and greater than they are now. He was of the children of Brogan, uncle of Milesius, and his brothers were Fuad and Eadar and Breagh, and all these being very great men are commemorated in the names of noble mountains and sea-dividing promontories."

"Guide thither the horses," said Cuculain. "It is right that those who take the road against an enemy should first spy out the land, choosing judiciously their point of onset, and Slieve Modurn yonder commands a most brave prospect."

Laeg did so. There, in a green valley, they unharnessed the horses and tethered them to graze, and they themselves climbed the mountain and stood upon the top in the most clear air. Thence Laeg showed him the green plain of Meath extending far and wide, and the great streams of Meath where they ran, the Boyne and the Blackwater, the Liffey and the Royal Rye, and his own stream the Nanny Water, clear and sparkling, which was very dear to Laeg, because he had snared fish there and erected dams, and had done divers boyish feats upon its shores.

Cuculain said, "I see a beautiful green hill, shaped like an inverted ewer, on the south shore of the Boyne. There is a noble palace there. I see the flashing of its lime-white sides, and the colours of the variegated roof and around it are other beautiful houses. How is that city named O Laeg, and who dwells there?"

"That is the hill of Temair," answered Laeg, "Tara's high citadel. Well may that city be beautiful, for the seat of Erin's high sovereignty is there. The man who holds it is Arch-king of all Erin."

"Westward by south," said Cuculain, "I see another city widely built, and unenclosed by ramparts and defensive works, and hard by there is a most smooth plain. At one end of the plain I see a glittering, and also at the other,"

And Laeg said, "That is the hill of Talteen, so named because the mother of far-shooting Lu, the Deliverer, is worshipped there, and every year, when the leaves change their colour, games and contests of skill are celebrated there in her honour. So it was enjoined on the men of Erin by her famous son. Chariot races are run there on that smooth plain. The glittering points on either side of it are the racing pillars of burnished brass, the starting-post, and that which the charioteers graze with the glowing axle. Many a noble chariot has been broken, and many a gallant youth slain at the further of those twain. It was there that Concobar raced his steeds against the woman with child, concerning which things there are rumours and prophesyings."

So Cuculain questioned Laeg concerning the cities of Meath, and concerning the noble raths and duns where the kings and lords and chief men of Meath dwelt prosperously, rejoicing in their great wealth. Cuculain said, "None of these kings and lords and chief men whom thou hast enumerated have at any time injured my nation, and there is not one upon whom I might rightly take vengeance. But I see one other splendid dun, and of this thou hast said no word, though thrice I have questioned thee concerning it."

Laeg grew pale at these words, and he said,

"What dun is that, my master?"

Cuculain said, "O fox that thou art, right well thou knowest. It is not a little or mean one, but great, proud, and conspicuous, and vauntingly it rears its head like a man who has never known defeat, but on the contrary has caused many widows to lament. Its white sides flashed against the dark waters of the Boyne, and its bright roofs glitter above the green woods. There is a stream that runs into the Boyne beside it, and there are bulwarks around it, and great strong barriers."

Laeg answered, "That is the dun of the sons of Nectan."

"Let us now leave Slieve Modurn," said Cuculain, "and guide thither my horses, for I shall lay waste that dun, and burn it with fire, after having slain the men who dwell there."

Then Laeg clasped his comrade's knees, and said, "Take the road, dear master, against the royalest dun in all Meath, but pass by that dun. The men are not alive to-day who at any time approached it with warlike intent. Those who dwell there are sorcerers and enchanters, lords of all the arts of poison and of war."

Cuculain answered, "I swear by my gods that Dun-Mic-Nectan is the only dun in all Meath which shall hear my warlike challenge this day. Descend the hill now, for verily thither shalt thou fare, and that whether thou art willing or unwilling."

Now, for the first time, his valour and his destructive wrath were kindled in the soul of Dethcaen's nursling. Laeg saw the tokens of it, and feared and obeyed. Unwillingly he came down the slopes of Slieve Modurn, and unwillingly harnessed the horses and yoked the chariot, and yoked the horses. Southwards, then, they fared swiftly through the night, and the intervening nations heard them as they went. When they arrived at the dun of the sons of Nectan it was twilight and the dawning of the day. Before the dun there was a green and spacious lawn in full view of the palace, and on the lawn a pillar and on the pillar a huge disc of shining bronze. Cuculain descended and examined the disc, and there was inscribed on it in ogham a curse upon the man who should enter that lawn and depart again without battle and single combat with the men of the dun. Cuculain took the disc from its place and cast it from him southwards. The brazen disc skimmed low across the plain and then soared on high until it showed to those who looked a full, bright face, like the moon's, after which, pausing one moment, it fell sheer down and sank into the dark waters of the Boyne, without a sound, or at all disturbing the tranquil surface of the great stream, and was no more seen.

"That bright lure," said Cuculain, "shall no more be a cause of death to brave men. This lawn, O Laeg, is surely the richest of all the lawns in the world. Close-enwoven and thick is the mantle of short green grass which it wears, decked all over with red-petalled daisies and bright flowers more numerous than the stars on a frosty night."

"That is not surprising," said Laeg, "for the lawn is enriched and made fat by the blood that has been shed abundantly now for a long time, the blood of heroes and valiant men - slain here by the people of the dun. Very rich too, are the men, both on account of their strippings of the slain, and on account of the druidic well of magic which is within the dun. For the people come from far and near to pay their vows at that well, and they give costly presents to those sorcerers who are priests and custodians of the same."

"Noble, indeed, is the dun," said Cuculain. "But it is yet early, for the sun is not yet risen from his red-flaming eastern couch, and the people of the dun, too, are in their heavy slumber. I would repose now for a while and rest myself before the battles and hard combats which await me this day. Wherefore, good Laeg, let down the sides and seats of the chariot, that I may repose myself for a little and take a short sleep."

For just then precisely an unwonted drowsiness and desire for slumber possessed Cuculain.

"Witless and devoid of sense art thou," answered Laeg, "for who but an idiot would think of sweet sleep and agreeable repose in a hostile territory, much more in full view of those who look out from a foeman's dun, and that dun, Dun-Mic-Nectan?"

"Do as I bid thee," said Cuculain. "For one day, if for no other, thou shalt obey my commands."

Laeg unyoked the chariot and turned the great steeds forth to graze on the druidic lawn, which was never done before at any time. He let down the chariot and arranged it as a couch, and his young master laid himself therein, composing his limbs and pillowing tranquilly his head, and he closed his immortal eyes. Very soon sweet slumber possessed him. Laeg meanwhile kept watch and ward, and his great heart in his breast continually trembled like the leaf of the poplar tree, or like a rush in a flooded stream. The awakening birds unconscious sang in the trees, the dew glittered on the grass; hard by the royal Boyne rolled silently. The son of Sualtam slumbered without sound or motion, and the charioteer stood beside him upright, like a pillar, his grey bright eyes fixed upon the house of the sorcerers, the merciless, bloody, and ever-victorious sons of Nectan, the son of Labrad.

Of the people of the dun, Foil, son of Nectan, was the first to awake. It was his custom to wander forth by himself early in the morning, devising snares and stratagems by which he might take and destroy men at his leisure. He was more cruel than anything. By him the great door of the dun, bound and rivetted with brass, was flung open. With one hand he backshot the bar, which rushed into its chamber with a roar and crash as of a great house when it falls, and with the other he drew back the door. It grated on its brazen hinges, and on the iron threshold, with a noise like thunder. Then Foil stood black and huge in the wide doorway of the dun, and he looked at Laeg and Laeg looked at him. The man was ugly and fierce of aspect. His hair was thick and black; he was bull-necked and large-eared. His mantle was black, bordered with dark red; his tunic, a dirty yellow, was splashed with recent blood. There were great shoes on his feet soled with wood and iron. In his hand he bore a staff of quickbeam, as it were a full-grown tree without its branches. He being thus, strode forward in an ungainly manner to Laeg, and with a surly voice bade him drive the horses off the lawn.

"Drive them off thyself," said Laeg.

He sought to do that, but owing to the behaviour of the steeds, he desisted right soon, and turned again to Laeg.

"Who is the sleeping youth?" said he, "and wherefore hath he come hither in an evil hour?"

"He is a certain mild and gentle youth of the Ultonians," replied Laeg, "who yester morning prosperously assumed his arms of chivalry for the first time, and hath come hither to prove his valour upon the sons of Nectan."

"Many youths of his nation have come hither with the same intent," said the giant, "but they did not return."

"This youth will," said Laeg, "after having slain the sons of Nectan, and after having sacked their dun and burned it with fire."

Foil hearing that word became very angry, and he gripped his great staff and advanced to make a sudden end of Laeg first, and then of the sleeper, Laeg, on his side, drew Cuculain's sword. Hardly and using all his strength, could he do so and at the same time hold himself in an attitude of defence and attack, but he succeeded. His aspect, too, was high and warlike, and his eyes shone menacingly the while his heart trembled, for he knew too well that he was no match for the man.

"Go back now for thy weapons of war," he cried, "and

all thy war-furniture, and thy instruments of sorcery and enchantment. Truly thou art in need of them all."

When Foil saw how the enormous sword flashed in the lad's hand, and saw the fierceness of his visage and heard his menacing words, he returned to the dun. The people of the dun were now awake, and they clustered like bees on the slope of the mound, and in the covered ways beneath the eaves and along the rampart, and they hissed and roared and shouted words of insult and contumely, lewd and gross, concerning Laeg and concerning that other youth who slept in such a place and at such a time. But Laeg stood still and silent, with his eyes fixed on the dun, and with the point of his sword leaning on the ground, for his right hand was weary on account of its great weight. Very ardently he longed that his master should awake out of that unreasonable slumber. Yet he made no attempt to rouse him, for it was unlawful to awake Cuculain when he slept. Conspicuous amongst the people of the dun were Foil's brethren, Tuatha and Fenla, Tuatha vast in bulk, and Fenla, tall and swift, wearing a mantle of pale blue. Around Fenla stood the three cup-bearers, who drew water from the magic well, Flesc, Lesc, and Leam were their names. At the same time that Foil reappeared in the doorway of the dun, fully armed and equipped for battle, Cuculain awoke and sat up. At first he was dazed and bewildered, for divine voices were sounding in his ears, and fleeting visionary presences were departing from him. Then he heard the people how they shouted and saw his enemy descending the slope of the dun, sights and sounds indeed diverse from those his dreams and visions. With a cry he started from his bed, like a deer starting from his lair, and the people of the dun fell suddenly silent when they beheld the velocity of his movements, the splendour of his beauty, and the rapidity with which he armed himself and stood forth for war.

"That champion is Foil, son of Nectan," said Laeg, "and there is not one in the world with whom it is more difficult to contend both in other respects and chiefly in this, that there is but one weapon wherewith he may be slain. To all others he is invulnerable. That weapon is an iron ball having magic properties, and no man knows where to look for it, or where the man hath hidden it away. And O my dear master, thou goest forth to certain death going forth against that man."

"Have no fear on that account," said Cuculain, "for it has been revealed to me where he hides it. It is a ges to him to wear it always on his breast above his armour, but beneath his mantle and tunic. There it is suspended by a strong chain of brass around his neck. With that ball I shall slay him in the manner in which I have been directed by those who visited me while I slept."

Then they fought, and in the first close so vehement was the onset of Foil, that Cuculain could do no more than defend himself, and around the twain sparks flew up in showers as from a smithy where a blacksmith and his lusty apprentices strongly beat out the red iron. The second was similar to the first, and equally without results. In the third close Cuculain, having sheathed his sword, sprang upwards and dashed his shield into the giant's face, and at the same time he tore from its place of concealment the magic ball, rending mightily the brazen chain. And he leaped backwards, and taking a swift aim, threw. The ball flew from the young hero's hand like a bolt from a sling, and it struck the giant in the middle of the forehead below the rim of his helmet, but above his blazing eyes, and the ball crashed through the strong frontal bone, and tore its way through the hinder part of his head, and went forth, carrying the brains with it in its course, so that there was a free tunnel and thoroughfare for all the winds of heaven there. With a crash and a ringing, armour and weapons, the giant fell upon the plain and his blood poured forth in a torrent there where he himself invulnerable had shed the blood of so many heroes. Laeg rejoiced greatly at that feat, and with a loud voice bade the men of the dun bring forth their next champion. This was Tuatha the second son of Nectan, and the fiercest of the three, he buffeted his esquires and gillas, while they armed him, so that it was a sore task for them to clasp and strap and brace his armour upon him that day, for their faces were bloody from his hands, and the floor of the armoury was strewn with their teeth. That armour was a marvel and astonishment to all who saw it, so many thick, hard skins of wild oxen of the mountains had been stitched together to furnish forth the champion's coat of mail. It was strengthened, too, with countless bars and rings of brass sewed fast to it all over, and it encompassed the whole of his mighty frame, from his shoulders to his feet. The helmet and neckpiece were one, wrought in like manner, only stronger. The helmet covered his face. There was no opening there save breathing slits and two round holes through which his eyes shone terribly. On his feet were strong shoes bound with brass. To any other man but himself this armour would have been an encumbrance, for it was good and sufficient loading for a car drawn by one yoke of oxen; but so clad, this man was aware of no unusual weight. When they had clasped him and braced him to his satisfaction, and, indeed, that was not easy, they put upon him his tunic of dusky grey, and over that his mantle of dark crimson, and fastened it on his breast with a brooch whose wheel alone would task one man's full strength to lift from the ground.

Then Tuatha went forth out of the dun, and when his people saw him they shouted mightily, for before that they had been greatly dismayed, and cast down on account of the slaying of Foil, whom till then they had deemed invincible. They were all males dwelling here together in sorcery and common lust for blood. No woman brightened their dark assemblies and the voice of a child was never heard within the dun or around it. So they rejoiced greatly when they beheld Tuatha and saw him how wrathfully he came forth, breathing slaughter, and heard his voice; for terribly he shouted as he strode down from the dun, and he banned and cursed Cuculain and Laeg, and devoted them to his gloomy gods. Beneath his feet the massive timbers of the drawbridge bent and creaked.

Said Laeg, "This man, O dear Setanta, is far more terrible than the first, for he is said to be altogether invulnerable and proof against any weapon that was ever made."

"It is not altogether thus," said Cuculain, "but if the man escapes the first stroke he is thenceforward invincible, and surely slays his foe. Therefore give into my hand Concobar's unendurable and mighty ashen spear, for I must make an end of him at one cast or not at all."

Tuatha now rushed upon Cuculain, flinging darts, of which he carried many in his left hand. Not one of them did Cuculain attempt to take upon his shield, but altogether eluded them, for now he swerved to one side and now to another, and now he dropped on one knee and again sprang high in air, so that the missile hurtled and hissed between his gathered feet. Truly since the beginning of the world there was not, and to the end of the world there will not be, a better leaper than thy nursling, daughter of Cathvah; and behind him all the lawn was as it were sown thick with spears, and these so buried in the earth that two-thirds of their length was concealed and a third only projected slantwise from the green and glittering sward. When the man with all his force, fury, and venom had discharged his last shaft and seen it, too, shoot screaming beneath the aerial feet of the hero, he roared so terribly that the shores and waters of the Boyne and the surrounding woods and groves returned a hollow moan, and, laying his right hand on the hand-grip of his sword, he rushed upon Cuculain. At that moment Cuculain poised the broad-bladed spear of Concobar Mac Nessa and cast it at the man, who was now very near, and came rushing on like a storm, having his vast sword drawn and flashing. That cast no one could rightly blame whether as to force or direction, for the brazen blade caught the son of Nectan full on breast under the left pap and tore through his thick and strong armour and burst three rib bones, and fixed itself in his heart, so that he fell first upon his knees, stumbling forward, and then rolled over on the plain and a torrent of black blood gushed from his mouth and nostrils.

"That was indeed a brave cast," said Laeg, "for the coat is the thickness of seven bulls' hides, and plated besides, and the rib-bones, through which Concobar's great spear impelled by thee hath burst his victorious way, are stronger than the thigh-bones of a horse; but pluck out the spear now, for it is beyond my power to do so, and stand well upon thy guard, for the two combats past will be as child's play to that which now awaits thee. Fenla, the third son of Nectan, is preparing himself for battle. He is called the Swallow, because there is not a man in the world swifter to retreat, or swifter to pursue. He is more at home in the water than on the dry land, for through it he dives like a water-dog, and glides like an eel, and rushes like a salmon when in the spring-time he seeks the upper pools. Greatly I fear that his challenge and defiance will be to do battle with him there, where no man born of woman can meet him and live."

"Say not so, O Laeg," said Cuculain, "and be not so afraid and cast down, but still keep a cheerful heart in thy breast and a high and brave countenance before the people of the dun. For my tutor Fergus paid a good heed to my education in the whole art of war and especially as to swimming. He is himself a most noble swimmer and I have profited by his instructions. Once he put me to the test. It was in the great swimming bath in the Callan, dug out, it is said, by the Firbolgs in the ancient days, and the trial was in secret and its issue has not been revealed to this day. On that occasion I swam round the bath holding two well-grown boys in my right arm and two in my left, and there was a fifth sitting on my shoulders with his hands clasped on my forehead, and my back was not wetted by the Callan. Therefore dismiss thy fear and answer thou their challenge with a strong voice and a cheerful countenance."

Laeg did that and he answered their challenge with a voice that rang, striking fear into the hearts of those who heard him. Forthwith, then, Fenla, wearing sword and shield, sprang at a bound over the rampart and foss, and his course thence to the Boyne was like a flash of blue and white and he plunged into the dark stream like a bright spear, and diving beneath the flood he emerged a great way off, and cried aloud for his foe.

"I am here," cried Cuculain, at his side. "Cease thy shouting and look to thyself, for it is not my custom to take advantage of any man."

Marvellous and terrible was the battle which then ensued between these champions. For the spray and the froth and the flying spume of the convulsed and agitated waters around that warring twain, rose in white clouds, and owing to the fierceness of the combat and the displacement of the waters around them, the Boyne on either hand beat her green margin with sudden and unusual billows, for the divine river was taken with a great surprise on that occasion. Amid the roar of the waters ever sounded the dry clash of the meeting swords and the clang of the smitten shields and the ringing of helmets. Sometimes one champion would dive seeking an advantage, and the other would dive too, in order to elude or meet the assault. Then the frothing surface of the stream would clear itself, and the Boyne run dark as before, though the mounted water showed that the combat still raged in its depths. The swallows, too, had been scared away, returning, skimmed the surface, and the bird which is the most beautiful of all darted a bright streak low across the dark water. Anon the submerged champions, coming to the surface for breath, renewed their deadly combat amid foaming waters and clouds of spray. The full particulars of this combat are not related, only that the wizard-champion grew weaker, while his vigour and strength continued unabated with the son of Sualtam, and that in the end he slew the other, and in the sight of all he cut off his head and flung it from the middle Boyne to the shore, and that the headless trunk of

Fenla, son of Nectan, floated down-stream to the sea. When the people of the dun saw that, they brake forth west-ward and fled. Then Cuculain and Laeg invaded the dun, and they burst open the doors of the strong chambers, and of the dungeons beneath the earth, and let loose the prisoners and the hostages and the prepared victims, and they broke the idols and the instruments of sorcery, and filled in the well. After that they replenished the vacant places of the war-car with things the most precious and such as were portable, and gave all the rest to the liberated captives for a prey. Last of all they applied fire to the vast dun, and quickly the devouring flames shot heavenward, fed with pine and red yew, and rolled forth a mighty pillar of black smoke, reddened with rushing sparks and flaming embers. The men of Tara saw it, and the men of Tlatga, and of Tailteen, and of Ben-Eadar, and they consulted their prophets and wizards as to what this portent might mean, for it was not a little smoke that the burning of Dun-Mic-Nectan sent forth that day.

CHAPTER XVI

THE RETURN OF CUCULAIN

"The golden gates of sleep unbar
When strength and beauty met together
Kindle their image like a star
In a sea of glassy weather."

SHELLEY.

Then Laeg harnessed the horses and yoked the chariot. To the brazen peaks of the chariot he fastened the heads of Foil and of Tuatha, with Foil's on the left hand and Tuatha's on the right; and the long-haired head of the water-wizard he made fast by its own hair to the ornament of silver that was at the forward extremity of the great chariot pole. When this was done, and when he had secured his master's weapons and warlike equipments in their respective places, the youths ascended the chariot, and Laeg shook the ringing reins and called to the steeds to go, and they went, and soon they were on the hard highway straining forward to the north. The sound of the war-car behind them outroared the roaring of the flames. Cuculain was a pale red all over, for ere the last combat was at an end that pool of the Boyne was like one bath of blood. His eyes blazed terribly in his head, and his face was fearful to look upon. Like a reed in a river so he quaked and trembled, and there went out from him a moaning like the moaning of winds through deep woods or desolate glens, or over the waste places of the earth when darkness is abroad. For the war-fury which the Northmen named after the Barserkers enwrapped and inflamed him, body and spirit, owing to those strenuous combats, and owing to the venom and the poison which exhaled from those children of sorcery, that spawn of Death and Hell, so that his gentle mind became as it were the meeting-place of storms and the confluence of shouting seas. A man ran before him whose bratta on the wind roared like fire, and there was a sound of voices calling and acclaiming, and a noontide darkness descended upon him and accompanied him as he went, and all became obscure and shapeless, and all the ways were murk. And the mind of Laeg, too, was disturbed and shaken loose from its strong foundations.

"But now," said Cuculain, "there ran a man before us. Him I do not see, but what is this herd of monstrous deer, sad-coloured and livid, as with horns and hoofs of iron? I have not seen such at any time. Lurid fire plays round them as they flee."

"No deer of the earth are they," said Laeg. "They are the enchanted herd of Slieve Fuad, and from their abode subterrene they have come up late into the world surrounded by night that they may graze upon Eiriu's plains, and it is not lawful even to look upon them."

"Pursue and run down those deer," said Cuculain.

"There is fear upon me," said Laeg.

"Alive or dead thou shalt come with me on this adventure, though it lead us into the mighty realms of the dead," cried Cuculain.

Laeg relaxed his hands upon the reins and let the steeds go, and they chased the enchanted herd of Slieve Fuad. There was no hunting seen like that before in Erin. So vehement was the chase that a twain of the herd was run down and they upon their knees and sobbing. Cuculain sprang from the chariot and he made fast one of the deer to the pole of the chariot to run before, and on to the hinder part of it to run behind. So they went northward again with a deer of the herd of Hell running before them and another following behind.

"What are those birds whiter than snow and more brilliant than stars," said then Cuculain, "which are before us upon the plain, as if Heaven with its astral lights and splendour were outspread before us there?"

"They are the wild geese of the enchanted flocks of Lir," answered Laeg. "From his vast and ever-during realms beneath the sea they have come up through the dim night to feed on Banba's plains. Have nought to do with those birds, dear master."

Cuculain stood up in his chariot with his sling in his hand, and he fitted thereto small bolts, and slang. He did not make an end before he had overthrown and laid low three score of the birds of Lir.

"Go bring me those birds," said he to Laeg. The horses were plunging terribly when he said that.

"I may not, O my master," said Laeg. "For even now,

and with the reins in my hand, I am unable to restrain their fury and their madness, to such a degree have their noble minds been disturbed by the sorcery and the druidism and the enchantment with which they are surrounded. And I fear that soon the brazen wheels will fail me, or that the axle-tree will fail me by reason of their collidings with the rocks and cliffs of the land, when the horses shall have escaped from my control and shall have rushed forth like hurricanes over the earth."

Forthwith Cuculain sprang out in front of the chariot, and seized them by their mouths and they in their rearing, and with his hands bowed down their heads to the earth, and they knew their master and stood still while they quaked. Laeg collected the birds, and Cuculain secured them to the chariot and to the harness. The birds returned to life and Cuculain cut the binding cords, so that the birds flew over and on either side of the chariot, and singing besides.

In that manner, speeding northward, Cuculain and Laeg drew nigh to Emain Macha. Concobar and the Ultonians happened at that very time to be seeking a druidic response from the prophetess Lavarcam concerning Cuculain and concerning Laeg, for their minds misgave them that beyond the mearings of the Province the lads had come to some hurt, and Lavarcam, answering them, said:

"Look to yourselves now ye children of Rury, Your destruction and the end of your career are at hand. Close all gates, shoot every bar. For Dethcaen's nursling, Sualtam's son, draweth nigh.

Verily he is not hurt, but he hath wounded. Champions

the mightiest he hath victoriously overthrown. Though he come swiftly it is not in flight. Take good heed now while there is time. He cometh like night in raiment of darkness, Starry singing flocks are round his head, Soon, O Concobar, his unendurable hand will he upon you; Soon your dead will outnumber your living."

"Close all the gates of Emain," cried Concobar, "and treble-bar all with bars. Look to your weapons ye heroes of the Red Branch. Man the ramparts, and let every bridge be raised."

So the high king shouted, and his voice rang through the vast and high dun and rolled along the galleries and far-stretching corridors, and was heard by the women of Ulla in their secluded chambers. And at the same time the watchman from the watch-tower cried out. Then the women held council together, and they said:

"Moats and ramparts and strong doors will not repel Cuculain. He will surely o'erleap the moat and burst through the doors and slay many."

And as they debated together they said that they alone would save the city and defeat the war-demons who had Cuculain in their power. For they said - "His virginity is with him, and his beautiful shamefastness, and his humility and reverence for women, whether they be old or young, and whether they be comely or not comely. And this was his way always, and now more than formerly since young love hath descended upon him in the form of Emer, daughter of Fargal Manach, King of Lusk in the south."

Then the women of the Ultonians did a great and memorable deed, and such as was not known to have been done at any time in Erin.

They bade all the men retire into the dun after they had lowered the bridge; and when that was done three tens of them, such as were the most illustrious in rank and famous for accomplishments, and they all in the prime of their youth and beauty, and clad only in the pure raiment of their womanhood, came forth out of the quarters of the women, and in that order, in spite of shame they went to meet him. When Cuculain saw them advancing towards him in lowly wise, with exposed bosom and hands crossed on their breasts, his weapons fell from his hands and the war-demons fled out of him, and low in the chariot he bent down his noble head. By them he was conducted into the dun, into a chamber which they had prepared for him, and they drew water and filled his kieve, and there Laeg ministered to him. He was like one fiery glowing mass - like iron plucked red out of the furnace.

When he had entered his bath the water boiled around him. After he had bathed and when he became calm and cool Laeg put upon him his beautiful banqueting attire, and he came into the great hall lowly and blushing. All were acclaiming and praising him, and he passed up the great hall and made a reverence to the King, and he sat down at the King's footstool. All who saw him marvelled then more at his beauty than at his deeds. He was sick after that, and came very near to death, but in the end he fell into a very deep sleep from which he awoke whole and refreshed, though it was the opinion of many that he would surely die. Cuculain was seventeen years of age when he did these feats.